SCOURGE OF THE SOUTH

The problems and cultural upheavals, around the time of the Civil War, would vastly change the Indian's ways ... When the Sioux swept down on the wagon train from the hills — only two people remained alive, Big Jim Ratford and twelve-year-old Sam Strake. They captured Sam, and ten years later he became a warrior, living a good life. But trouble loomed. The whites wanted their land — the buffalo herds were slaughtered, and in desperation the Indians sued for peace ...

GEORGE HOLT

◆

SCOURGE OF THE SOUTH

Complete and Unabridged

LINFORD
Leicester

First published in Great Britain in 2000

First Linford Edition
published 2010

British Library CIP Data

Holt, George, *1919* –
  Scourge of the south.
  - - (Linford western library)
  1. Western stories.
  2. Large type books.
  I. Title II. Series
  823.9'14–dc22

  ISBN 978–1–44480–166–8

Published by
F. A. Thorpe (Publishing)
Anstey, Leicestershire

Set by Words & Graphics Ltd.
Anstey, Leicestershire
Printed and bound in Great Britain by
T. J. International Ltd., Padstow, Cornwall

This book is printed on acid-free paper

1

For three days now the ominous column of smoke had risen from the dark hills to the north, and everyone in the wagon train was jumpy and on edge with tension. It affected them all, each in their different way; the outriders were taciturn and glanced often to the hills, the settlers checked and rechecked their guns, tested their harness and tried to goad the patient oxen to even greater speed, the women fussed and snapped at the children, their faces haggard and drawn with strain. Even the wagon boss, big, bearded Jim Ratford had lost his ready smile, and his eyes, as he stared at the grim plume, held anxious fears for the safety of those he led.

'Think we'll make it, Jim?' Curt Walhen, tanned, dressed in the skins and equipment of a trapper, reined in his horse and walked it beside that of the wagon boss.

'Maybe,' said Jim. shortly. 'Maybe not.' He turned in his saddle and stared back at the wagon train. Behind him, wending snake-like over the plain, the great Connestoga wagons looked what they were, ships of the desert. Each wagon was drawn by teams of oxen, yoked in pairs, six, eight, or ten to each wagon. Water barrels were fastened to the sides of the high, wooden bodies, together with spare wheels, shovels, axes and other tools. Inside the wagons rested the stores and seeds, household goods and certain pieces of prized furniture which the settlers had carried all the way from the East. Some of the wagons had horses trailing behind them, their reins looped to the back-boards, and a couple even had cows. They were the signs of those wagons which held newborn babies and, watching them, Big Jim frowned.

'Tell number five to speed it up,' he called to an outrider. 'Close up the train and tell the drag to stay in close.'

The man nodded and, wheeling his horse, galloped down the line to relay the order. He, like the wagon boss, knew that there would be no argument. Independent as the settlers were, yet they had banded together for mutual protection and knew that the safety of all rested on implicit obedience to the wagon boss.

Big Jim frowned at the column of smoke and rubbed thoughtfully at his beard.

'Three days is a long time,' he said, more to himself than to the man at his side. 'Maybe that smoke is just a warning not to settle down in Sioux territory, and then again maybe it ain't.'

'Want for me to take a couple of the boys and do a scout?' Curt Walhen shifted in his saddle and glanced behind him. 'I could take Luke and Mark, both of them are good at scouting and I reckon they could be spared for a couple of days.'

'If the Indians attack we won't be

able to spare a man,' said Big Jim curtly. 'There are too many women and children in this train for my liking. Too many women and not enough fighting men. If we are attacked we're going to be in trouble.'

'The women can handle a rifle as well as the men,' said Curt defensively. He himself belonged to the train, unlike Big Jim, who had been hired as boss back in Fort Henry, and whose responsibility would be over when they reached California. 'I reckon we can show those red devils a thing or two if they should get the wrong ideas about us.'

'Maybe.' Big Jim didn't argue the point. He had guided too many wagon trains across the seemingly limitless plains of the Mid-West to have any doubts as to the danger of the Indians. The Sioux were plains Indians, warriors, and they had a fanatical dislike of the settlers which, like a never-ending stream, pushed in from the East.

Curt changed the subject as he

jogged along. 'When we left Fort Henry there was talk of a Civil War, you think there's anything in it?'

'Could be.' Big Jim rode as he always rode, seemingly relaxed, but his eyes beneath their shaggy brows were never still. A rabbit could have jumped from behind a rock and he would have seen, aimed the Colt at his waist and killed it before another man would have noticed it. He leaned forward and automatically loosened the Sharps rifle in his saddle scabbard. It was a gesture meaningless in itself, but typical of the man. To be instantly ready for any emergency was the strict code by which he lived.

'Funny to hear talk of war,' said Curt. 'It don't seem possible somehow. Why should men go to war when there is all the land anyone could want out here for the taking? You'd think that they'd have better sense.'

'When men argue about something neither of them understand, you can't expect them to have sense,' said Big Jim drily. 'Me? Well, I don't aim to worry none about the quarrel between the North and South. I'm a Westerner and I'm going to stay that way!'

'All this fuss about a bunch of darkies,' continued Curt. 'So what if a few of them do slip their chains and run North? It don't hurt no one, does it?'

'Maybe you'd feel differently if it was your property that was on the run,' said Big Jim drily. 'Maybe you'd think like the South, that all slaves should be handed back to their owners. Or would you be an abolitionist? You sure talk like one.'

'What if I am?' Curt stared at the big man, his eyes defiant. 'I don't see why any man should be bought and sold like a mule, and the fact that he's got a dark skin don't make no difference. They're human, ain't they?'

'Did I say they wasn't?'

'No, but most people seem to think that way, and that's what this talk of war is all about.'

'You're wrong,' said the wagon boss quietly. 'I don't know much and I don't say much, but I was talking to a lawyer fella a while ago and he explained it all to me as plain as could be. Seems that this question of the runaway slaves is only part of it. This is a big country, Curt, but it ain't big enough to have two governments at the same time. The South are getting a mite too cocky and they are trying to tell the rest of us what to do. Sure, I reckon that a slave owner feels bad about it when his property runs off to the North and he can't get them back, but that's no call to threaten if the North won't do as he says. And then the North ain't lily-white about it. Most Northerners don't give a bent cent for the slaves, but they don't like the South, and so they scream that slavery is all wrong and should be stopped.'

'Well, shouldn't it be?'

'I'd say yes, but that don't mean I'd go to war about it.'

'Then how else would you stop it?'

'I don't know. I reckon that if a man wants to do something then he's got a right to do it without interference from others.' Big Jim shrugged. 'Maybe I've lived out West too long to think different, but it don't seem right to me that white men should fight among themselves when the Indians are still scalping and raiding as they wish. Seems that it would be a good idea to get together and put the Indians in their place, so that decent folk could ride the plains without worrying about their hair.'

He turned and frowned back down the line of wagons.

'What's the matter with number five? I told that rider to tell them to pull up; hell, with a gap like that between the wagons we'll be in trouble for sure if that smoke means anything.'

Without waiting for the other man the wagon boss wheeled his horse and galloped back to the offending wagon. Turning, he rode beside the dashboard and touched his hat to the woman who held the reins.

'You'll have to move faster, Mrs

Strake. I sent a man back to tell you that a while ago; did he?'

'He did,' admitted the woman. She was thin, dressed in faded calico and poke bonnet, and her hands as she held the reins were gnarled and knotted with too-hard work for too long a period. 'I'm sorry, Jim, but I can't seem to get any speed out of these animals.'

'You need a rider to goad them up a bit,' said Big Jim. 'Ain't you got a man, madam?'

'My man's dead,' she said without emotion. 'He died back at Fort Henry and I'm alone with my boy.'

'So?' Big Jim frowned a little. He remembered the incident, the man had been crushed to death when falling from the wagon in a drunken stupor, and against his better judgment he had permitted the woman to join the train with her son. He looked into the wagon.

'Where's your boy. ma'am?'

'Back with the Fenshaws.' She didn't make any comment, but the set of her thin lips showed how she felt.

'The Fenshaws?' Big Jim dragged at his reins. 'I'll get him for you, Mrs Strake, and use the whip on them oxen; unless you manage to keep up I'll have to put you back at the end of the line, we can't risk the train for a single wagon.'

He was being hard and he knew it, but he knew too that there was nothing else he could do. Logically the slowest wagon should be in the front and the fastest in the rear. Sometimes the drag was reserved as a punishment spot, for following the others it collected all the dust thrown up before it and was the most uncomfortable spot in the train, even though the wagons did not move in a straight line, but were staggered so as to miss the dust thrown up before them. But this was Indian country and they had to move fast. The lead wagon set a brisk pace and it was up to the others to keep up with it or fall behind. If they fell behind it wouldn't matter, not if they were the last wagon, not matter to the rest that is.

But Big Jim hated losing a woman from any of his trains, and his face, as he rode towards the Fenshaws' wagon, was grim.

'Is young Strake in there?' he called as he approached the wagon.

'Sure!' Mark Fenshaw, a smiling, easy, good-natured man of about forty, looked back into the wagon and called something.

'You want me?'

Young Strake was about twelve and old for his years. He had inherited his father's indifference and little of his mother's will to work. He leaned indolently on the side of the wagon, chewing a straw, his eyes insolent as he stared at the wagon boss.

'Climb on back of me,' snapped Big Jim. He waited while the youngster threw a leg over the horse behind him, then spurred out of earshot. 'Listen, Sam, and listen good. You're a big boy now, almost a man, and you've got to act like as if you was all grown up now that your Pa's dead. Your Ma is in trouble with her wagon and needs you. Now, I know that you ain't all bad inside and I know that it gets boring just sitting up there handling the reins, but it's got to be done. So how about riding with your Ma and seeing that she don't get into trouble?'

'She said that I wasn't wanted,' said young Sam sullenly. 'I can't help it if she don't want me.'

'Your Ma is a proud woman,' said Big Jim patiently. 'She don't want to beg no favours, but I'm telling you different. She needs you beside her now more than ever.' He pointed towards the thin column of smoke on the distant horizon. 'See that?'

'The smoke? Sure. Indian sign, ain't it?'

'Sioux sign. They don't like us coming into their territory and they may decide to do something about it. If they do then we're going to be in trouble. If they attack we'll have to move fast and act quick. Your Ma's a good woman, Sam, but I'm thinking that a man should be in charge of that wagon, not a female. You get what I mean?'

'Yes.' Sam had lost his sullenness as he grasped what the wagon boss was trying to say. 'You want for me to protect her, is that it?'

'That's it, Sam. You got a gun?'

'Pa's rifle is in the wagon and I can use it.' Sam stared again at the column of smoke. 'You think that the Indians will attack?'

'I ain't saying,' said Big Jim, slowly. 'But they don't send up smoke for nothing.' He spurred his horse towards the head of the train. 'I'll drop you off and you get your wagon up close.' He winked at the boy, knowing just what he was doing. 'Between you and me, Sam, women are peculiar creatures. They got to be handled just right and they need a lot of patience. Understand?'

'Sure.' Sam hesitated as they approached his wagon. 'I wasn't aiming to be ornery, Jim, but you know how it is.'

'I know.'

'A woman forgets that a boy grows up into a man, and tends to treat him like a kid.' Sam hesitated, his youthful face reflecting his thoughts. 'I guess that I've been a little impatient.'

'That's what I figured,' said Big Jim, and managed to restrain himself from smiling. 'Now don't forget, Sam, I'm relying on you.'

'I won't let you down.' Sam took the reins from his mother and sent the long thong of the whip cracking over the heads of the lead oxen. 'Move, you varmints!' he yelled in his clear, boyish voice. 'Move!'

Big Jim didn't smile until he was back at the head of the train, and even then he didn't smile for long. Men grew fast on the frontier, and at twelve a boy was almost a man. He could ride, fend for himself and kill his enemy. He could work from dawn to dusk seven days a week, and often had to, and, as in Sam's case, family responsibility came all too soon. Sam, despite his age, was a man.

Big Jim hoped that he would continue to act like one.

Curt Walhen was waiting, and the trapper had news.

'Jud just rode in from scout and says that he saw a big group of Indians. He ducked out of sight before they saw him.'

'Where is he?'

'I sent him back for chow, he was all in.'

'Fetch him.' While waiting, Big Jim called to an outrider. 'Collect the boys and stay close to the train. Move up all wagons. use force if you have to, but get them tight. Move!'

'Trouble, Jim?' The other hesitated, his face anxious.

'Maybe, maybe not, but we want to be ready for it just in case.'

He followed the man with his eyes as he rode off, glad that he himself owned neither wagon, goods, nor had a family. His responsibility was great enough, without having to worry about his kinfolk, but he could sympathize with those who had their wives and children, their goods and all they owned in the wagon train. He shrugged off the thought as Curt returned with the scout.

'Curt tells me that you saw some Indians,' snapped Big Jim. 'Where?'

'About ten miles north of here.' The scout wiped crumbs from his mouth and spat in the dust. 'I reckon there were forty-fifty of them.'

'Painted?'

'Yeah. Feathers, war-paint, the works.' The man spat again. 'All braves and all mounted. They was heading direct north, away from us.'

'Did you see their paint? Were they Sioux?'

'I guess so. I don't know much about Indians, but they sure looked as if they meant business. I waited until they were gone and then rode back here. I didn't wait to see if I could spot any game, I guessed that food could wait.'

'You were right.' Big Jim stared up at the sun, his eyes thoughtful. 'Almost noon and time to rest.' He glanced back at the train. 'No sense in wearing ourselves out before we have to, and the beasts need water.' He lifted his arm and sent a shrill, long drawn-out cry into the air. 'Train — halt!'

'Tell the riders to set out posts and keep watch. Let them ride out a couple of miles and return as soon as they spot anything moving,' he said to Curt. 'Pass the word to water and feed the beasts. No cooking fires, we must eat cold.'

'Right.' Curt was moving away when Big Jim called him back.

'And Curt.'

'Yes?'

'Tell the men to keep their guns handy. Don't make a big thing of it, tell them privately, but tell them.'

'I get it.' Curt lifted his hand in salute and rode away. Big Jim scratched at his beard as he stared towards the horizon.

'You think that they'll attack, Jim?' Jud stared towards the horizon and looked anxious. He had a wife and three children in the train, one of the children barely able to crawl. He'd lost his two

17

brothers in Indian raids and knew what to expect. He, like most of the settlers, saw nothing romantic in fighting Indians, all he wanted to do was to reach California without trouble.

'Not here,' said Big Jim with a conviction he wished he felt. Indians, he knew, could attack in any locality, but looking around he felt sure that they were as safe as could be expected.

All around stretched the vast plains of the Mid-West, mile on unbroken mile of short grass, browned now and burned by the searing heat of the summer sun. To the north the hills showed as a looming cloud of darkness against the clear blue of the sky. To the south and east the arid plain stretched to the horizon, while to the west it ended in a mass of scrub and chapparal. Big Jim had guided the train with experienced skill, and if the Indians were to attack now he would have plenty of warning. Now. Later on would be something quite different.

A few miles to the west the plain gave

way to low foothills and relatively dense underbrush. That lasted for a few miles until the spring he was heading for had passed and the plain began again stretching, this time to the arid reaches of the desert, beyond which lay the great barrier of the Rockies.

The danger point was obviously the foothills, with their shielding under-brush, which would hide an attack. But Jim, as he knew, could be wrong, and it was with his usual caution that he rode out from the halted wagons to take a look at what lay ahead. He had barely gone a furlong when someone called to him, and turning he saw young Sam Strake, mounted on a borrowed horse, spurring towards him.

'You going out on a scout Jim?'

'Something like that!' Big Jim looked stern. 'I thought we agreed that you were to stay with your Ma?'

'She said that I could go for a ride. Luke said he'd lend me his horse.' Sam looked wiser than his years. 'I think that Luke has a shine on Ma and wanted to get me out of the way.'

It was possible and, as Jim had to admit, it would be a good thing if Luke, himself a widower, would join up with Mrs Strake. Mourning was soon over and done with in the West. Life was too hard to permit the luxury of grief, and it took a man to build a house, break new ground and put in a crop. It took a man to do that and a woman to tend house, grind flour, milk the cows, if any, and to do the thousand and one things essential for survival. Widows were scarce on the frontier, and the few who managed to remain unwed earned little but contempt.

He hesitated, his eyes scanning the horizon, and Sam mistook his hesitation for reluctance to ride with him.

'If you can't be bothered with me, Jim,' he said with a dignity beyond his years, 'just say so. I don't aim to stay where I ain't welcome.'

'Did I say that?' Big Jim was quick to sense the hurt he had caused. 'I just wondered whether you'd be able to stand the pace if I have to let her go. We might have to ride in a hurry, Sam, and I'd rather not have to stop to pick you up.'

'I can ride,' said Sam, a little mollified. 'Can I ride with you, Jim? Can I?'

Big Jim hesitated again, thinking it over. There was no really good reason why he should not let the boy accompany him and plenty of good ones why he should. If Luke was serious about tying up with the widow the quicker they sealed it the better. They could be married by the preacher accompanying the wagon train, and if he kept Sam out of the way while the couple talked it over, the whole thing could be settled at the next camp.

'Come on then,' Big Jim ordered curtly. 'No tricks and no shouting. We're on a scout so we want to see without being seen. Get me?'

The boy nodded and silently, aside from the beat of their horses' hooves, they rode over the plain towards the scrub ahead. Big Jim felt his nerves tighten as they neared it, and with his automatic gesture leaned forward to loosen the Sharps rifle in its boot. Satisfied that it rested easily to hand, he drew his Colt and spun the chamber, checking to see that every chamber held its cartridge. Sam watched him, his eyes alight with envy.

'Gee!' he said, 'I wish that I owned a gun like that.'

'Didn't your Pa have a gun?'

'Sure, but not one of those hand guns. All he had was an old rifle.' Sam sounded disgusted. 'A muzzle loader at that. Guess Pa never thought much of shooting.'

'Where are you from, Sam?'

'Kentucky.'

'They make good guns down that way,' said Jim. quietly. 'You've probably got one of the old-time squirrel rifles, easy to manage and accurate up to a hundred yards.'

'Maybe, but I'd like one of the new ones, a Sharps or one of them Henrys I've seen the soldiers carry. But most of all I'd like one of them Colts, the new ones which take the cartridges like you've got. Better still, I'd like two.'

'What for?' Jim smiled as he stared at the boy. 'If you can't kill a man with one gun, you're not likely to do it with two.' He spun the chamber again and slipped the weapon back into its holster. 'Know much about guns, Sam?'

'Some. Why?'

'I've got an old revolver back in my duffle. One of the percussion cap loaders. She's accurate and a reliable firer so long as you keep the powder dry. Like it?'

'You'd give it to me?'

'Maybe.'

'What you want in trade?' Sam was suspicious. The gun Big Jim had mentioned was the forerunner of the Colt he himself carried, slower to load but just as lethal in an experienced hand. Sam was not to know that, for practical purposes, it had been rendered obsolete by the newer cartridge-loading types now coming into the West.

'Nothing. You just act good on the trip and I'll give it to you.' Big Jim winked. 'Maybe I'll let you carry it during the ride; you can practise some if you've powder and ball and caps. Have you?'

'Sure, Pa had a boxful of them, he bought them cheap when we started out.' Sam stared ahead into the distance. 'You mean that, Jim?'

'Yes.'

'Right, it's a deal. I know what you're aiming at and I'll play along.' He hesitated. 'I suppose you know that I don't have to be paid to do my duty by Ma?'

'I know'

'If you thought that I'd rather not take the gun.' Sam's reluctance was obvious. 'I'd sure like to have a pistol of my own, but — '

'Stow it!'

'What?'

'Stow it. Button your lip!' Big Jim's voice reflected his tension. Sam, instinctively obeying, stared around him as he tried to find out the need for silence.

'Back slow,' whispered Big Jim. 'Wheel and ride easy and gentle. Keep close to me and, when I give the word, ride as if all hell was after you back to camp.' He grinned without mirth. 'I ain't joking, either, all hell is right.'

'Indians?'

'Yeah. Look over there, behind that tree, see?'

'No.' Sam, looked, but could see nothing but the foliage. 'That bird, you mean?'

'That ain't no bird,' whispered Big Jim. 'That's a feather from a war bonnet. Now take it easy, if they guess we've spotted them they'll perforate us with arrows before we can wink. Slow and easy, that's it, slow and easy.'

He raised his voice as they urged their horses in a slow, lazy turn. 'Nothing here, Sam, so I reckon we may as well push on through.' Incredibly he chuckled. 'Fancy yourself as a rider, don't you? Well, I'll bet a plug of tobacco that I reach camp before you do. Ride!'

Desperately Sam thudded his heels against the ribs of his horse.

2

For a moment nothing happened, and Sam, clinging desperately to the reins of his galloping horse, thought that they had got away with it. Then something whistled over his shoulder to stick quivering in the ground before him. Something else tugged at his sleeve and he heard Big Jim curse. Then the air was full of the most horrible screaming he had ever heard, and the Indians, shrieking their war-whoops, boiled from the foothills behind them.

Sam risked one quick glance backwards, then, driving his heels against the ribs of his mount, clung to the reins and concentrated on nothing but speed. Behind him, mounted on their wiry ponies, came the Indians. There were about a dozen of them, painted in grotesque patterns, feathered and daubed for war. They screamed and shrieked as they rode, waving their lances and coup sticks, a few with rifles bought from traders or won in raids, but most with the bow and arrows with which they were so skilled. They rode barebacked, their sinewy legs gripping their mounts as they fitted arrow to string and fired from the saddle. Fortunately for Sam and Big Jim, their start had soon put them beyond arrow range, and by the same token they were out of the effective range of the rifles also. But the Indians were the more skilled riders, their ponies capable of great bursts of speed, and it was only a matter of time before the two were ridden down.

'Give it all you've got, boy.' Big Jim spoke through clenched teeth, the painted arrow sticking out from his left arm mute testimony as to his pain. 'Ride like hell or we're done for for sure.'

'Can we make it?' Sam could think of nothing but clinging to the horse and the Indians behind him. 'Have we got a chance?'

'We're alive, ain't we?' Big Jim turned in the saddle and swore as he saw that the Indians had decreased their lead. 'Hell! The devils are gaining on us.'

It was true. The braves had stopped screaming now that their initial surprise was over. The sole purpose of their war-whoops was to paralyse their enemy with fear, but now that they were on the chase they had fallen silent. Big Jim swore again as an arrow flashed beside him.

'They'll perforate us soon. Ride, Sam, faster!'

'I'm all out,' gasped Sam. 'The horse can't run any faster.'

'That's what you think,' snapped Big Jim. He twisted awkwardly in his saddle and the short quirt in his hand whined down across the animal's flank. It seemed to give a great bound and then, incredible as it seemed to the boy, it was galloping even faster than before. Frantically he clung to the mane of the horse, the ground beneath seeming to blur as he watched it, all detail lost in a green-brown haze. Again the wagon boss lashed the horses and again they seemed to gain new strength from the cruel sharpness of the pain, but it was a temporary strength, neither animal was in top condition and both had been worked hard during the past few days. Suddenly Sam knew that unless a miracle happened they would be ridden down long before they reached the safety of the camp.

Big Jim thought so too. He turned and snarled as he saw how near the Indians had come, then dragging the Colt from his belt he triggered three quick shots towards them. He missed, he hadn't really hoped to do anything else, but as he triggered the last three shots towards the pursuers, the roar of his pistol was answered from ahead.

'The outriders!' Sam stared at them as if hardly able to believe his eyes. 'We're saved!'

A dozen men came galloping towards them, riding hard, their heads low and their hands weighed with pistols. The air became filled with sharp snapping sounds, and from the Indians came a terrible screaming as they saw their prey escaping. Without pause Big Jim and Sam rode directly towards the rescue party, through them, and slowed down only when the dying yells of the Indians told them that their pursuers had turned tail and fled. Curt Walhen, his face split by a grin, rode up to the wagon boss.

'Reckon we was just in time,' he said easily. 'It was lucky that Jud decided to ride out a piece after you.' He chuckled as he thrust fresh cartridges into his pistol. 'I guess we made them Indians sorry they started anything.'

'Get any?'

'No, but we sure scared them plenty.'

'That's what you think.' Big Jim scowled at the arrow transfixing his arm. 'Jud, ride on to the camp and warn them to expect an attack, Curt, cut out this arrow for me, will you?' He swore as Curt prodded at the shaft. 'Hell, let it ride. Let's get those wagons circled for the attack.'

'You think that they'll attack now?' Walhen sounded dubious. 'From the look of them they won't stop running this side of the hills.'

'They were an advance party waiting in ambush,' said Big Jim. He rode as he spoke, his eyes anxious. 'They've gone back to tell the main party.' He rose in his saddle and stared towards the hills. 'Look!'

'I can't see anything.'

'Look again. Down below that bluff. See?'

Sam stared in the indicated direction and felt his heart jump within him. A shadow moved there, a dark patch of moving shape which, even as he watched, grew larger. The dull thunder of beating hooves filled the hot air as Big Jim spurred his mount towards the camp.

'Circle!' he yelled. 'Get them wagons moving. Fast!' The rest of his words were lost in the yelling of men and the lowing of oxen.

It was a manoeuvre which the train had often practised before. Quickly, to the accompaniment of cracking whips and yelling men, the sluggish oxen broke into a lumbering run, dragging the heavy wagons behind them. For a few minutes all was confusion, and then the dust settled to show the wagons arranged in a neat circle, the oxen unharnessed and resting within the circle, the outriders jumping their mounts over the shafts to stand ready with their rifles.

'Water barrels and buckets ready,' ordered the wagon boss. 'Get those kids in the wagon bodies where they'll be safe. You men take cover and wait for the signal. You women stand by to help the wounded, load the guns and shoot if you can. Move!'

He gritted his teeth from the pain of his wound, and Sam, standing beside him, caught his eye.

'Help me, Sam,' said Big Jim. 'Take my bowie and cut away my sleeve.' He bared his teeth as Sam operated the knife, scared lest he should cause pain. 'Get on with it, boy, don't be afraid of hurting me.' He grinned with agony as Sam cut and ripped away the sleeve. 'Good. Now get me the whiskey from my duffle in the lead wagon.'

'What are you going to do?' Sam returned with the whiskey and looked at the painted shaft sticking from the brawny arm. 'Cut it out?'

'I'll show you.' Tilting his head, Big Jim took a swallow of whiskey then poured some liberally over his arm, washing the blood from the wound. 'There are two ways to get an arrow out, Sam. You can cut it out or pull it through. If this was a hunting arrow I'd just pull it out, but this is a war arrow, one with a barbed head. If it was in the body you'd cut off the shaft and leave it there until a doctor could attend to it. That's if you wanted to. Me, I like to get it over and done with.' He took another drink of whiskey. 'Cut off the shaft about six inches from the wound. Right, now we shove it through.'

Sam felt sick as he watched the big man grip the shaft, hesitate, then press on it until the barbed head of the arrow came out of the other side of his arm. Quickly he gripped the arrow head, pulled and reeled back against a wagon, sweating with pain.

'The whiskey,' Jim gasped. 'Quick, Sam, the whiskey!'

He gripped the bottle and drank the potent spirit as though it had been water. He gasped, then deliberately he poured the raw spirit over and into his wound.

'Get me a clean piece of linen, a shirt tail or a strip from a sheet, and bind up my arm good and tight.'

'I'll attend to it,' said a new voice, and Sam looked up to see his mother. Deftly she bound the wound with a prepared bandage, and watched as Big Jim gulped more whiskey.

'That stuff don't help none,' she said tartly. Big Jim grinned.

'Perhaps not, ma'am,' he admitted. 'But it sure helps a man to forget his misery.' He set down the bottle, inspected his bandage and nodded. 'Thank you, Mrs Strake, that's a real neat bandage. I guess you've attended to a wound before.'

'Often.' She looked worried. 'What's going to happen now, Jim? The Indians after us?'

'Yes.' He pointed towards the hills. 'Here they come, you can see their paint now, they'll strike at any moment.' He turned, and his voice rang over the camp. 'Stand by for trouble. Here they come!'

They came like a horde of painted devils, grotesque in their warpaint, their feathers making them look something less than human and their war-whoops adding to that impression. They came in a solid charge, shooting a hail of arrows, firing their few rifles, hurling their lances. They came as if they intended to ride over the wagons, and that was their intention. Big Jim ruined it by his sharp command.

'Let 'em have it!'

Fire burst from the wagons, from beneath the wagons, from the wheels and from every bit of cover the great wooden bodies offered. A hail of smoke and lead driving the foremost ranks of the Indians into a broken shambles, sending ponies and warriors to sprawl on the blood-soaked grass, filling the air with the roaring thunder of exploding powder.

Again the volley rang out, again, a fourth time and a fifth, then the firing became ragged as men aimed at individual targets, firing and loading with desperate haste as Indian after Indian shrieked and yelled and rushed towards the wagons. Smoke drifted from the circle, the thick grey smoke of burnt powder — and through the shielding mist the Indians seemed more than ever like the red devils they were called.

Then the charge broke and the firing died as the settlers counted their losses.

They were too many. Men and women, children too, lay sprawled in death, their bodies bearing the feathered marks of arrows or the red-fringed wounds of lance or bullet. Luke was dead, Mr Fenshaw, his eldest son, others. Many others, and staring at them Big Jim glowered his hate towards the Indians. They had taken to circling the wagons, riding their ponies around and around in a circle just beyond effective rifle range, and the wagon boss knew that they would so circle until, abruptly, they would swing in closer for another charge.

'Get the wounded in the wagon beds,' he ordered. 'Men, collect up the weapons and load them ready for use. Get those kids under cover, the bigger ones can stand by with water buckets.'

'Afraid of fire, Jim?' Curt Walhen, his face speckled with burnt powder, looked anxiously at the canvas tops of the wagons. 'You think that they'll try fire arrows?'

'Sure they will, just as soon as they get round to it.'

Big Jim glared at the circling shapes.

'There aren't many tricks the Sioux don't know about, unpleasant ones mostly, things like letting a man die slow or stretching him out with rawhide thongs. You know about that?'

'I've heard tell of it,' said Curt sombrely. 'They stake a man out tight with wet rawhide. When the thongs dry they shrink.' He shuddered. 'I want a clean death and that means that I'm not aiming for those red devils to take me alive.' He spat and cleared his throat. 'Think we can beat them off?'

'We'd better,' said the wagon boss grimly. He glanced around and lowered his voice. 'Listen, Curt, you've been around this part before and you know a thing or two about the Sioux. Most of these folk don't. I don't want anyone getting the wrong ideas about coming to terms with them or anything like that. We kill or get killed. Understand?'

'Sure, you don't have to tell me.'

'Then pass the word.' The wagon boss looked up as a shrill yell came from a lookout.

'Get ready! Here they come!'

This time the Indians did not charge blindly at the wagons. They had learned their lesson and so, instead of rushing directly into the guns, they circled nearer to the wagons and within rifle and arrow range. They fired from the backs of their galloping ponies, showing superb skill in handling their mounts, but the settlers were in no mood to admire that skill.

'Pick your targets,' yelled the wagon boss. 'Aim slow and steady. Don't waste your bullets.' He crouched beside Sam where he was aiming his dead father's rifle. 'Don't waste time with that gun now, Sam. Pick yourself a carbine, there are plenty of them around now, and don't get excited.' He nodded to Mrs Strake. 'Get the women loading for the men, ma'am, and stay under cover.'

'You don't have to tell me what to do Jim,' she snapped. 'How's that arm?'

'Giving me hell,' he admitted. He whipped the Colt from his belt and fired at an Indian lying a few yards away. 'Playing possum,' he explained grimly. 'I could see him sweat, and dead men don't sweat. He was aiming to wriggle close in the excitement and collect a scalp or two.' He blew down the barrel of his pistol. 'He ain't playing now, though.'

Mrs Strake looked sickly. Frontier woman though she was, yet the sight of blood had always upset her, even though she managed to hide her weakness before others. Now, to cover her feelings, she began to bustle about the space between the wagons, organizing the water bucket detail, the bandages, telling off the other women to their duties and seeing that everyone knew what they had to do. She was bending over a wounded man when the arrow struck her between the shoulders.

Sam saw it. He saw the coloured flash and the feathered shaft ringed with blood as it tore into his mother's lungs. He saw her straighten, heard her scream then Big Jim was beside him, holding him down despite his struggles.

'Stay where you are and keep firing.' He thrust the boy back against his wheel and shoved a carbine in his hands. 'She's gone, Sam. there's nothing you can do for her now, but get the red devil who did it. Get him, Sam. Get him and a dozen more.'

'But — '

'She's dead, I tell you. Dead as a doornail, I've seen it happen before.' His harsh voice softened as he looked at the boy. 'It was quick, Sam, quick and clean. She didn't even know what hit her.'

It was a lie. There is nothing quite so painful as an arrow wound, especially one with a barbed head with its ripping, tearing impact, but the rest of what he had said was true. Death had been quick, a flash of agony, the shocked realization of what had happened, then blackness and the end. More important was that Sam should not dwell on his grief. For one thing it would serve no purpose and, for another, every man, woman and child capable of aiming a gun and pulling a trigger was needed to beat off the Indians.

Sam gulped and, lifting the carbine to his shoulder, aimed and pulled the trigger. The recoil almost broke his shoulder, and the bullet whined away into the distance.

'Not that way, Sam.' Big Jim opened the breech and thrust in another cartridge. He didn't seem to notice that his wounded arm was dripping blood. 'Aim steady and hold her tight to your shoulder. Follow your target and squeeze gentle. Squeeze, Sam, don't pull, and keep following your target.' He grinned as Sam obeyed his instructions. 'That's better.' Now try again, take your time, Sam, one dead Indian's worth a dozen holes in the air. 'Ready, now!'

Sam fired, a warrior screamed and toppled from his pony, and Big Jim slapped the boy on the shoulder. 'You've got it! Now knock 'em down as they come.'

He lost his grin as he crawled from

under the wagon and looked about the circle of wagons. The Indians had kept up a remorseless fire, and though they, too, had suffered, yet the settlers had suffered more. Dead sprawled from the wagons, hanging limply over the shafts of the great wagons, hunched behind wheels and twisted on the ground. The canvas tops were riddled with holes and feathered with arrows, and the moans of the wounded sounded above the continuous thud of horses, the whoops of the Indians and the rattle of ceaseless gunfire.

Big Jim glanced up at the sky and was surprised to see that the sun was far down towards the horizon. It didn't seem possible that the battle had already lasted for several hours, but his own fatigue and the stench of burnt powder around him told him that it must be so. He stooped and squinted at the circle of Indians, firing with his pistol at the painted shapes as they passed. It took good marksmanship to hit them, and it took even better marksmanship for them to hit the settlers. It is easier to hit a moving object from a stationary platform than a stationary target from a moving platform, and had all things been equal the settlers would have won outright. But they were not equal and the settlers didn't stand a chance.

They were concentrated in a tight area, and every arrow and bullet fired by the Indians into that area had a chance of hitting living flesh. If enough missiles were aimed, then inevitably enough of the defenders would die so as to make the final charge easy. Big Jim knew the procedure of Indian fighting and knew, too, that with well-armed men he could have fought and won. But he was hampered with women and children without enough horses to mount sufficient men to make a sortie, and all he could do was to sit and wait and hope that, after enough of them had been killed, the Indians would give up and leave the train in peace.

Then what he had feared most

happened in a soaring point of flame and smoke.

'Fire arrows!' Curt Walhen, his face blackened beyond recognition, an ugly gash marring one cheek, stared at the point of flame and smoke. 'Jim! They're using fire arrows!'

'I expected it,' said the wagon boss. 'They must have hoped for plenty of loot to have held them off this long.' He snarled as fire began to lick over one of the canvas tops. 'Water buckets! Douse that fire, quick!'

Even as he snapped the order more arrows winged towards the wagons and within seconds a dozen points of flame leapt and smoked from woodwork and canvas.

'We've got to put out those fires.' Curt swayed and grabbed at a bucket. He darted towards a water barrel, filled the bucket and tossed the water on to the smouldering canvas. He dipped again, turned, them slumped as a thrown tomahawk smashed in his skull.

'Stay in your positions!' yelled Big

Jim. 'Never mind the fires, stay at your positions and get ready for the next charge.'

He might as well have spoken to the wind. As the fires spread, the screams of the wounded rose above the roar of guns and as they saw the creeping flames and felt their heat, they grew desperate at the thought of being burned alive. No one could have heard their prayers and remained aloof. Men and women dropped their guns and raced to rescue those caught in the burning wagons. Girls and boys worked like mad things as they drained the water barrels and flung the precious liquid over the crackling woodwork. Big Jim stormed among them, his hands clenched into fists as he knocked them away and back to their guns.

'Fools! You're doing just what the Indians want. Let them burn! Let the wagons burn!'

'I can't.' A man, his face singed and blackened, caught at Jim as he passed. 'All I own is in that wagon. If I lose it then I'm ruined. I — '

'You fool! What are goods when you're dead? Get back to your position and forget the wagons. Get back, I say!'

Somehow he beat sense into them. Somehow, despite the storm of arrows which lanced through the smoke, the bubbling cries of those writhing in their death agonies and the screams of the burning wounded, he lashed them back to their guns. He was only just in time.

They came with a dreadful pounding of hooves and a screaming, blood-curdling war-whoop. They raced at the wagons like painted devils, their lances flashing before them and their tomahawks swinging in their hands. Some died. Some shrieked as they felt the bite of lead and fell, to be trampled beneath their pony's hooves, but the rest came on.

And suddenly they were through the barrier and riding among the burning wagons.

Sam still crouched beneath a wagon, shooting his carbine through the spokes of a wheel, saw them charge and had time to fire one shot before they had crashed through. He rolled from beneath the wagon, his eyes smarting from the smoke of the burning timbers, and was almost knocked down as a pony brushed against him. To one side he saw Big Jim, a reversed rifle in his hands, smashing at shaved skulls and painted faces in a desperate fury not to be taken alive. Sam dodged as a warrior thrust at him with his lance, slipped on a pool of blood, and grabbed at the reins of a horse which whinnied above him.

Frantically he climbed up into the saddle, snatched at a second pair of reins and, with little or no plan, rode directly towards where Big Jim stood and battled for his life. All around him screams and shrieks made the air hideous with sound. Indians, screaming and yelling, rode down unarmed women and children, lancing and tomahawking, jumping from their ponies to take a scalp or a colourful scrap of clothing. Men, their faces desperate with the knowledge that they had nothing to lose, stood and fought until they were literally hacked to pieces. The Indians seemed to have lost all control of themselves, they fought and howled and killed without regard to age or sex.

But Sam took no notice of the noise and confusion around him. He had eyes only for Big Jim himself and, as he drove forward, the wagon boss saw him and suddenly redoubled his efforts. The rifle splintered as it pulped a skull, the jagged end was thrust into the face of an Indian, who, tomahawk lifted high, was poising for the throw, the barrel cracked across the face of a third and, without pause, the big man sprang into the empty saddle beside Sam.

'Ride!' he snapped. 'Quick!'

Sam nodded and followed the big man. The wagon boss rode like a man possessed, he dug in his spurs, sent his mount rearing against a knot of Indians, and then he was galloping towards the ring of burning wagons, had jumped the shafts and was headed towards the open plain beyond. Sam, rode after him, desperately clinging to the mane of his horse, while behind him rode a painted redskin, lance poised, the light of battle in his eyes.

Sam glanced as he saw him. Ahead, Big Jim neither looked back nor slowed, but crouched over his horse and rode as if all the devils of hell were at his heels. Twice Sam tried to call out, twice he could utter nothing but a croak, and then, as he tried for a third time, his horse stumbled and he went hurtling over its head to sprawl in a stunned heap directly before the charging Indian.

His last conscious memory was of a painted face, the bright tip of a lance, and the thunder of hooves as they rushed towards him.

3

Walking Dog, Shaman of the Sioux, stood before the village of tepees and watched as the line of returning warriors rode towards him. They rode silently as befitted grown men, and aside from the soft thud of their unshod ponies a slight clink or jingle as metal touched metal, and the subtle sounds of harness, they rode as if they were a ghost band. Walking Dog shielded his eyes and his lips moved as he stared at the warriors. He was counting them, and when he had finished his shoulders drooped a little before he turned to address the women.

'Many went,' he said evenly. 'Not so many have returned.'

They had expected it and so his statement came as no surprise. Always when the warbands rode out there were some who failed to return. Then the widows would rend their garments, paint their faces with charcoal and go off by themselves a little way. They would take all that had belonged to the dead man, his blankets and weapons, his charms and amulets, and they would bury them in a secret place. His name would never be mentioned, for to mention the name of the dead is to bring bad luck. After a brief while they would remarry or perhaps they would choose to remain widowed — no one would try to force them either way.

The line of warriors reached the village and halted, while the women ran up and down to see if they could recognize a familiar face. If they were fortunate their voices would lift to a high-pitched song of praise and they would run to their tepees, there to grease their hair and to paint their faces red and yellow, white and brown with coloured earth and crushed berries in the colours of gladness. Some did not see the expected faces, and these mourned and went off alone.

'Welcome back to the tepees of the Sioux,' said Walking Dog in his deep voice. His eyes flickered down the line and over the pack animals. 'You have met with success?'

'We have.' Great Bull, Chief of the Sioux and leader of the war-party, slipped down from his horse and, climbing a knoll, addressed the tribe. 'Many have gone to the Happy Hunting Grounds and these we mention but once and then no more. Walking Dog will call the names and then let them be as if they never were.' He waited while the shaman called out thirty names.

'Many of us have not returned to the lodges of our fathers, but more than that number of the white men lie for the birds of ill omen to feast upon their eyes. We have also brought many horses and saddles. Many guns and blankets. Much food and clothing for our women. We shall share these things tonight at the celebration.'

He spread his arms and the tribe

dispersed, all but one warrior, who rode up to the chief.

'The boy, Great Bull. He is mine?'

'That must be decided tonight at the Council Fire, Red Cloud,' said the chief.

'But I found him, he is mine.'

'He belongs to no one, and belongs to us all.' There was stern reproof in the even voice of the old chief. His tone softened as he stared at the warrior. 'A child is not a bow that he can be given or claimed. He is not a horse so that you can say he is yours. Tonight the decision will be made. I have spoken.'

The warrior hesitated, then nodding he walked away towards his tepee. Walking Dog touched the arm of the old chief.

'A prisoner?'

'Yes. Red Cloud took a young boy and desires him for his own. He has reason for his claim, but we must be certain we do the child justice.'

'True. But Red Cloud has no son. He would make a good father.'

'I know and he shall have the boy. But it is well for him to wait, haste often spoils the gourd, and the hunter who hurries often goes hungry.'

The shaman laughed at the old proverb and followed the chief into his tepee.

That night when the sky was thick with stars and the great Council Fire had been lit, the division of the spoils took place. Each member of the tribe joined the circle around the fire, the old men and squaws nearest the fire, then the young married women, the divorced women and those not yet wed. Then the warriors, the braves and the young boys who had not yet reached manhood. Between the ranked circles the children ran and shouted, played and acted as children do the world over.

Great Bull handed out the spoils, giving to each according to his need; a rifle to a warrior who had no gun, blankets to those who needed them, flour and bacon to the sick and aged. The Sioux, like all the plains Indians, took little heed of personal possessions. A man's wealth was not important, and mere possession did not make a warrior more important in the eyes of the tribe. The only time when a young brave needed possessions was when he bought a wife, then he would need horses and blankets, beads and rifles to give to her father so that she would be his. Even so, the women were not chattels in any sense of the word. They had the power to throw a bad provider from the tepee and, if they wished, they could return to their parents. In such a case a man had the right to demand back his gifts, but if he had been thrown from his tepee for non-providing, he earned only scorn and contempt from the others. He, too, could divorce his squaw and take another wife, though no Indian would do so unless by mutual agreement.

Finally, after the last of the plunder from the destroyed wagon train had been distributed, Red Cloud led forward the sole prisoner.

Sam was scared. He was only twelve years of age, and though he had hidden his fear during the battle, yet he felt his mouth go dry as he stared at the stern faces around him, looking even more stern and savage in the dancing light of the fire. He, like most boys of his age. had heard the tales of terrible tortures done to captives by the Indians and, as he was led forward, fully expected to be tied to a stake and burned alive. He tried to stand upright as Great Bull stared at him, shuddering a little as he saw Walking Dog, now wearing his ceremonial robes and carved mask. In the firelight the shaman looked totally inhuman with his elaborate headdress and grotesque mask.

'Be not afraid,' said Great Bull in English. 'You will come to no harm.'

Sam swallowed and wished that he could believe that. His last memories had been of a painted warrior bearing down on him, lance at the ready, and he still couldn't understand how it was that he was still alive. Fear, shock, and the fall had all helped to throw him into a merciful unconsciousness, and this, more than anything else, had caused Red Cloud to lift his lance at the last moment and capture instead of killing.

'You killed my Ma,' said Sam defiantly. 'You killed her and all the others.'

'When the arrow flies who knows where it may settle,' said Great Bull impassively. 'It is war. Your people die and our warriors die. We think no harm of you because of our empty tepees and our wailing women. Why do you think harm of us?'

'You asked for it,' said Sam. He stood a little straighter. 'You attacked us without reason.'

'This land is the land of the Sioux,' said the chief evenly. 'It is not the land of the white man. If a man breaks into your tepee and steals your blankets, would you not attack him? So, it is the same with us.'

'Give me the boy,' said Red Cloud impatiently. 'For many moons I have waited for a son, but my wife is barren and I have waited in vain. Laughing Water is a good squaw and I would not put her from my side. Give me the boy so that I may have a son.'

He spoke in the guttural tongue of the Sioux and Sam didn't understand a word of what he said.

'You shall have the boy,' said Great Bull. 'He shall be to you as your own and you shall teach him in the ways of our people.' He stared at Sam. 'You will not be harmed. Red Cloud, who is a great warrior, will take you into his tepee and teach you our ways, so that you may become one of us. From now your name will be Stone Face, and you will walk in our path as the son of Red Cloud. I have spoken.'

Sam was too young to realize the full implications of what the chief had said. He did not know that, to the Indians, adoption was perfectly common and done without regard for race or colour. Captured children were always given to those who had the greatest need and then brought up exactly as the other Indian children. Women captives, too, were adopted, usually they worked for a time as general servants, but could attain equal status with any other woman of the tribe if they took a warrior for husband. There was no compulsion, women were treated with distant courtesy, and most of them, after they had settled down, were only too pleased to enter fully into the life of the tribe.

Sam, though he didn't yet know it, was now almost a fully-fledged Indian.

Red Cloud took him to the animal skin tent which was his tepee and there handed him over to his wife, Laughing Water. She smiled at the serious face of the young white boy then, with a woman's sure instinct, fed him until he could eat no more and then wrapped him in a blanket to fall asleep. Later, when Sam rested in the deep, easy sleep of youth, she crept from the tepee to stand at the side of her husband.

'You have brought me a great gift,'

she said quietly. 'The boy is weak now, but soon he will become strong and be as other children. It is good, my husband.'

'He shall wear the skins of a young Sioux,' said Red Cloud. 'I shall give him a bow and together we will hunt in the hills. I shall teach him our tongue and how to ride without a saddle. He will wear paint and ride with me on the warpath. It is good!'

His arm closed around the slender shoulders of the woman at his side, and from his great hunger he spoke again.

'It is good!'

*   *   *

Sam's education as an Indian started immediately he awoke. He found that his clothes had gone to be replaced by fringed trousers and moccasins, a short leather jacket and a thong with which to tie back his hair. He donned them and joined the rest of the children as they ran down to the river to bathe. After his wash he ate a mess of pounded corn, meat and beans and then, his first fears gone, thought of a plan to escape.

But escape wasn't so easy.

The horses were guarded by warriors and he had no idea which path to take through the hills in order to reach a settlement or a fort. So, with a young boy's easy adaptability, he put off his intention to rejoin his own kind and made the best of what was offered to him.

An older man would have found it hard to forget himself so utterly as to begin to think and act like a natural-born Indian. Sam was only twelve, superficially hard, but inwardly only a child. His upbringing had been hard, kicks and curses from his drunken father and cold indifference from his overworked mother, and he found the genuine love and affection given him by his new parents irresistible. Also, like most boys of his age, he had a great desire to hunt and fish, learn bare-back riding and the use of bow and arrow, knife and tomahawk, rope and lance.

Each day he woke a little more Indian than the day before. He learned the Sioux tongue and laughed and played with the other boys of his age. Mostly he failed in any games of strength or skill, but as his chest deepened and his skin tanned, his muscles grew strong and he was able to hold his own.

The memory of a child is long, but his emotions are short-lived. Sam hadn't forgotten the wagon train, but now, to him, it seemed far away and almost unreal. Red Cloud was his father, Laughing Water his mother, Stone Face his name. It was an odd name for a boy who smiled almost all the time, but the Indians, with their peculiar sense of humour, thought it appropriate. Sam was so different to their own impassivity that they thought his name well chosen. And so time passed as he rode and hunted, dressed and talked as the other Sioux and neared the time when he, like all Indian boys, became a man.

Sam wondered about it and asked the shaman, Walking Dog, to explain it to him.

'Has not Grey Horse, your friend, told you of what is to come?' Walking Dog, older now, but still active, stared thoughtfully at the young man standing before him. Sam was almost an Indian, almost. As yet he wore no paint, that was reserved for the mature members of the tribe, and still dressed in the skins of a youth. His features betrayed his true origin, he had none of the stern dignity of the plains Indians — instead his eyes were blue, his hair a light brown, his nose and chin obviously that of a white man. His features made no difference to his acceptance as a full member of the tribe. He could have been a black man and he would still have been accepted. The Indians were not concerned with race, colour, or physical appearance. To them, the test of a man resided in his heart and his courage.

'Grey Horse is two years younger than I am,' said Sam. 'He goes for his initiation soon, why may I not also go, Walking Dog?' He spoke the tongue of the Sioux with easy familiarity and used the terms of respect normally saved for addressing chiefs and great warriors. Walking Dog smiled as he recognized the obvious flattery.

'Each boy receives his initiation when he is ready,' said the shaman. 'Grey Horse is ready. Are you ready?'

'I am.'

'So you say, and yet you are not an Indian born and have been with us for only a short space of time. You would become a warrior and ride the warpath against our enemies. You would wear paint and feathers and take a squaw, but these things do not make a boy into a man. That comes from within.'

'I am ready,' said Sam again.

'The rites are simple and yet must not be told,' continued Walking Dog. 'There is the test of courage, the test of honour, the test of faith. These tests you must pass. Manitou alone knows whether you can do so.'

'He will give me strength,' said Sam quietly. 'I am ready.'

'It is well. Your initiation will commence at the birth of the next moon. Inform Red Cloud that it is so. I have spoken.'

Red Cloud was jubilant when he heard the news, and even Laughing Water managed to hide her pain at losing the boy who was her son to gain a man who would be a warrior. She herself knew nothing of the rites, and Red Cloud, who knew them too well, did not speak of them. Instead he built a small shelter far from the village and told Sam that he must stay in it, alone and in communion with the spirits so that they would grant him their aid in the ordeal to come.

'Purge yourself of weakness, my son,' he said. 'Rest and let your thoughts dwell on the spirit world around us. The spirits are strong and they will aid you if they will.'

'What happens if I fail to pass the tests?' asked Sam.

'I shall be shamed,' said Red Cloud quietly.

'I shall not fail,' promised Sam.

'It is well. All take the tests to become men instead of boys, but with us each decides his own time. Remain a child a while longer if you wish, none shall blame you, but take the tests and fail and all shall regard you and those who are yours with shame. It is not well for a man, even a child, to boast of what he cannot do.'

'I shall pass,' said Sam again. 'I thank you, my father, but I shall pass.'

Alone he sat in the shelter and thought about the coming ordeal.

The initiation rites of the Sioux were similar to those followed by other tribes, varying only in detail. The entire purpose of the rites was symbolic and had a deep religious significance. It was a time when the child became a man, with all a man's rights and responsibilities. In no sense was it an escape from childhood. The childhood of an Indian was the happiest time of his life, for no adult was ever anything but kind to him. Physical punishment, any form of punishment for that matter, was unknown. Children were regarded as the most important members of the tribe and had any and everything they wanted. They were cherished and cared for to an incredible extent, with the result that each Indian had a deep sense of security. To him his tribe was his family, his home, his happiness. It was a feeling which he never lost during his life.

Sam had absorbed some of that feeling. His love for his adopted parents was very real, his earlier life but a shadowy memory, and yet that earlier life had robbed him of the very thing every Indian accepted as his right. Sam, despite his recent upbringing, did not have the deep abiding sense of security which his friend, Grey Horse, had. Sam was inclined to be restless, to worry, to wonder what would happen in the future. He did not have the calm acceptance of fate which the Indian had.

And so he sat and worried about the coming ordeal.

Grey Horse and a few of the other boys were taking their initiation at the present time. His own would commence at the birth of the moon, a few days from now. He knew that he had to pass successfully. He remembered the advice of his adopted father, Red Cloud, and smiling, settled himself for sleep.

Maybe the spirits would be kind to him.

4

The night of the new moon came and with it Walking Dog, the shaman of the Sioux. He came to the little shelter dressed in his robes and wearing his grotesque mask. He stood and called, and Sam, his senses tingling with anticipation, came out of the shelter and stood before him.

'Stone Face, you are ready?'

'I am ready.'

'It is well. You will follow me and make no sound. You will remove your moccasins, your trousers, your jacket. You will wear a loin cloth, carry your knife, and that is all. You will follow me and make no sound. It is understood?'

'It is understood.'

Sam did as he was bid, stripping down to a twist of cloth around his waist and carrying his knife in his right hand. The shaman stared at him, lifted his right arm as if at a signal, and walked towards the edge of the clearing. Barefoot and almost naked Sam followed him, remembering the repeated caution to make no sound.

He found out the purpose of the instruction as he trod on the leaf of a cactus.

The pain was sickening. The sharp spines drove deep into his sole and for a moment Sam almost cried out with the pain. He prevented himself just in time, remembering the warning he had been given. To make a sound now was to fail one of the tests. Silently he removed the spiney leaf and followed the figure of the shaman. Again he trod on a cactus, again he winced and almost cried out, again he removed the thing from his foot and hobbled on. Sharp stones dug at his feet as he walked, but his feet had grown hard and these he did not mind. What did trouble him was the thorny branches which lashed at his almost naked body.

Walking Dog had deliberately led the

way through a big clump of thorn bushes. He himself was protected by his thick, ceremonial robes, but Sam had no protection and, when he finally emerged from the bushes, his body was scored and lacerated in fifty places. The shaman halted at the top of a low mound.

'You have trod the path of pain and have made no sound. It is well. Now you must go out into the wilderness alone, armed but with your knife, and there you will stay until the moon has died and the new moon is born again. You will live as you might, eat as you may, drink where you can. You will remain until it is time for your return and you will speak to no man and no man must speak to you. Go!'

Painfully Sam hobbled into the darkness before him.

The test was both arduous and essential. Arduous because the initiate had to live on his own resources for a month, and essential because there would be many times in the life of a warrior when such knowledge would be important for him to know. Sam, armed only with a knife, his body a mass of scratches and lacerations, had to find shelter, catch game for food, drink water where he could find it, and live as best he might. He suddenly realized that if he failed he would not be able to return, and his failure would automatically bring his own death.

Grimly he struggled on into the darkness.

He spent the rest of that night huddled between two boulders, and woke, stiff and sore and raging with thirst. His thirst he managed to quench by licking the dew from the rocks, and after some exercise he rid himself of the stiffness in his muscles. The region where the shaman had left him was bare and desolate aside from the underbrush hiding the village where he dared not yet return. Instead, Sam struck out towards the horizon, and after walking for several miles sat down to make his plans.

He had to have food, water and shelter. He could do without fire, he could eat raw meat as well as cooked, and the weather, though cold with approaching winter, was not yet unbearable. Deliberately he sat down and remembered all the little seemingly innocuous trifles which he had been taught. Now he could see that, far from being a childish game, such teachings were literally life or death, and it was up to him to prove himself a man by managing to live.

From a stunted bush he made a crude bow and a handful of arrows, tipping them with heads chipped from stone. He made also a rabbit snare and some thongs of twisted bark. Night fell before he was finished, and again he huddled against a boulder, slaking his raging thirst on the collected dew. While a temporary expedient, dew was not enough, and as he suffered beneath the baking, mid-day sun, he knew that he must find water soon or perish.

He found it at the foot of a stunted tree, digging deep with his bare hands until he was rewarded by a small pool of liquid. That day, too, he caught a rabbit, knocking it over with his bow and arrows and slitting its throat with his knife. He gulped the blood, skinned the beast and ate it raw, licking his fingers to clean them after the meal.

Later he found a cave and set snares on the rabbit paths. He shot a bird, a tough and stringy buzzard, and once almost managed to shoot a small deer.

It was a hard, unrewarding life, but it served to make him fully aware of his own capabilities. It was during such initiation periods, he knew, that the spirit-guide of an Indian was supposed to manifest itself. Often this happened towards the last stages when, weak with hunger and privation, the initiate would seem to see a presence, speak with it and gain valuable advice as to the future. Then also was the tribal totem revealed to the individual, the sacred symbol of animal or bird which would be the initiate's religious totem during life. Then also did the normal Indian make his medicine bag, his sachet of lucky charms and tokens used to ward off evil spirits and bring good fortune.

Sam did not see any manifestations of the spirit world. He ate too well for that nor was he troubled by a totem symbol, the Sioux did not have such rigorous totem symbolism. But he did make a medicine bag.

He made it from the skin of the first rabbit he had killed, good fortune in that surely, and placed in it the arrowhead responsible for killing the beast, a handful of dried berries, a lump of rock streaked with peculiar yellow markings and unusually heavy, and a feather from the buzzard. Later he would add more things of special significance. Maybe a bullet which had almost, but not quite, killed him, a strand of hair from the head of a friend, or a carved charm won or found by some lucky chance. The contents of a medicine bag were peculiar to the individual. The general theme was that it brought good luck and warded off evil. The results depended both on the contents of the bag and the wearer's belief in it.

As the old moon died and the new moon was ready to be born he returned to the village.

Walking Dog met him and silently led him to the tribal fire. All the village had gathered and Sam found himself the centre of attention as he followed the shaman towards the leaping fire. Walking Dog halted, raised his arms and called on the spirits of the north, the south, the east and the west. He called on the Great Father, Manitou, and he called on the spirits of the Happy Hunting Grounds. He swept his arms in a circle, halted and pointed directly at Sam.

'Speak with a straight tongue. You have seen no man?'

'I have seen no man.'

'No man has spoken to you?'

'No man has spoken to me.'

'Were you aided by stealth or foresight?'

'I was aided by none.'

'You swear that for one moon you have lived alone and without aid from man or woman, child or demon, God or spirit?'

It was a trick question and Sam took his time before answering.

'I have lived alone aided by no living thing other than the beasts and birds sent to me by helpful spirits. Of this world I can answer, of the spirit world I cannot.' He knew that it was not the custom to question a returned initiate about any manifestations he may have seen. Such visions were regarded as private and, unless the returned initiate wanted to speak about them himself, none would pry.

'It is well.' The shaman spun and faced the fire, he turned again to Sam.

'This is the final test. If you lie then suffer for your lies. If you speak with a true voice you will not be harmed. Put out your tongue.'

Sam hesitated, then did as he was bid. He tensed as the shaman twisted to the fire and turned again, this time holding a glowing iron. Without pause he touched the hot metal against Sam's tongue.

'Warrior!' he shouted. 'He has passed!'

Immediately drums began to beat from the assembled Indians, and men and women began to caper in the intricate dance of welcome. After a while the women dropped out, and the men, warriors all, painted and daubed in their warpaint, feathered and decked as if for battle, danced to the beat of the drums as they welcomed Sam as a new member of their ranks.

Sam, still a little dazed by the whole proceedings, sat beside Red Cloud and watched the dance. He still couldn't understand why his tongue hadn't been severely burned when the shaman had touched it with the red-hot iron.

'The mouth of a man who lies and is guilty is dry with fear,' said Red Cloud when Sam asked the question. 'The iron burns — how it burns, and we know that the initiate has spoken with a forked tongue. The mouth of a man without fear is wet and the iron does not burn his flesh.'

It was the oldest lie test in existence, and fortunately for Sam it worked.

The dance lasted until the stars had faded and the sun painted the east with fingers of pink and gold, blue and yellow, orange and amber. Then the tired warriors departed to their tepees and Sam, because he was now a man and could no longer share the tepee of his parents, joined Grey Horse in the tepee set aside for the single men.

He slept until noon, then woke and washed in the river before joining the others around the communal pot of succotash. After he had eaten, Red Cloud called to him and presented him with a bow, a quiver full of arrows, a tomahawk and a rifle.

'These things are yours,' he said with simple pride. 'They are poor things which I have fashioned during the time of Ghost Face, when the world was frozen and the nights cold. The rifle came from the wagon train. Take them, my son, and ride against the enemies of our people.'

'Thank you, my father,' said Sam. 'I shall treasure these things you have given me.'

'They are as nothing to the joy you have brought to my tepee. There is a horse also, a good mount which I also give to you.' Red Cloud hesitated. 'There is nothing else. It is the custom, you understand?'

'I have lived with you and am of you,' said Sam quietly. 'You have given me a horse and weapons and the rest I must provide. I shall try to be brave in battle and collect many scalps to decorate my tepee, and,' he flushed a little, 'my wife, when I have one, will honour you and Laughing Water.'

'A warrior needs a wife,' said Red Cloud. 'A woman to prepare his skins and cook his food, to grind his corn and bear his children. Tell me, Stone Face, have you cast your eye on any young maid?'

'Can a boy look at women?'

'You are no longer a boy.'

'And not yet a warrior. Not until I have ridden with a war-party and earned the right to wear feathers can I be that. I shall speak of a wife when I am a man, not before.'

'You speak wisdom,' said Red Cloud, pleased at the answer. 'It is well.' He glanced to where the other young warriors stood. 'Grey Horse wishes to speak with you. You have wasted enough time in talk with an old man. See what he wants.'

'The words of my father are words of wisdom. To hear them is to learn. Grey Horse can wait.'

Red Cloud smiled a little at the respectful words and then pushed Sam towards the others.

'You speak with a tongue of honey. You will rise in the Council if you use words which turn the thoughts of men. See what Grey Horse wants.'

'Yes, Red Cloud.'

'Stone Face.'

'If it should come into your heart to take a wife,' said Red Cloud, and appeared to be very interested in a formation of cloud just overhead. 'If you should need a go-between and if the price be high, well, be not afraid to let me know. I have horses, many horses, and other things with which to win a bride. Need I say more?'

'To lean on the old tree makes a man weak when he needs to stand alone,' said Sam. 'To be a man, father, I must be a man. To be worthy of a wife I must win her without the help of those who have given me so much.'

'You speak bravely,' smiled Red Cloud. 'But you speak as a child. When the fire is in your blood and your tepee is but a place to leave as soon as you might, remember my words.'

'I shall remember them.'

'It is well. Go now and good hunting attend you.'

'And you, Red Cloud.'

Sam moved off and joined the impatient Grey Horse. The Indian was two years younger than Sam, but as they stood together the difference was hardly noticeable. Grey Horse was excited at some news he had just heard.

'A messenger rode in from the south with heavy tidings. He is talking to Great Bull now, but I crept to the tepee and heard what he had to say. There is war with the Apache to the south, great war, and I think that we must be ready to take the warpath against them. The messenger is from Black Eagle of the Cheyenne and they have great quarrel with the Apache.' Grey Horse chuckled. 'If we ride together then there will be many horses and fine blankets, much food and many guns and scalps.'

Sam nodded. He knew that there was almost constant warfare between the various Indian tribes and that raids were common. Such raids were conducted by a band of warriors who would swoop down on the enemy village, kill the men, steal the women and children, and take what they could. The main object of these raids was horses and goods to provide against the winter. Such warfare was not vicious in the sense that either side wanted to utterly destroy the other. In effect it was more of a game in which the young warriors could test their skill. Each individual raid was assumed to be a 'war' on its own and, as soon over was as soon forgotten. Many braves carried 'coup sticks', feathered shafts, each feather of which told of a successful coup or raid. Sam, naturally, was interested in taking a part, for as a warrior he was now entitled to ride with the men.

Grey Horse's information had been correct. The messenger from the Cheyenne had arranged with Great Bull for the use of some of his warriors to join Black Eagle on a raid against the strong tribe of the Apache in their stronghold in the southern desert.

The chief came out of his tepee and spoke to the assembled braves.

'Our brother of the Cheyenne has come to ask that many warriors of the

Sioux join with him against his enemy of the Apache. Cochise is the chief of the Apache and he is a brave man. You may have heard of Cochise!'

Sam had. The almost legendary figure of the chief had earned a reputation among the southern settlers and Mexicans. So great was their fear of him that the Mexicans called him the Scourge of the South and waged unremitting war against any of the Apache they could find. Terrible tales of horrible tortures done to both red man and white had filtered up to the Sioux and few indeed were the Mexicans who thought of the grim figure of the Indian chief without a muttered prayer for their own safety and a curse for the Indian.

'He is a great warrior,' continued Great Bull. 'He is strong in battle and fleet to attack. Our brothers of the Cheyenne have suffered much at his hands and desire to revenge themselves on him. I have said that you may go if you so wish it.'

Great Bull, like all Indian chiefs, had no real power to order a brave to do anything. He could persuade, request, but could never command in the same sense that a white officer could command his troops. Discipline to the Indians was a totally foreign concept. They did what they wanted when they wanted, and the only punishment the chief could give was to expel the offender from the tribe. Such a punishment was equal to exile and, to the Indian, far more serious than mere death. Even this punishment could only be given with the consent of the majority, a coward in battle, for example, a murderer or a warrior who earned the scorn and contempt of the others would be so punished. So Great Bull did not command the warriors to ride with the Cheyenne, he merely gave them permission to go should they so desire.

The response was immediate.

'I'll go,' said Grey Horse, and dragged Sam forward with him. 'And

Stone Face will go with me.'

'I'll go.' Another warrior stepped forward, and then came a rush of young braves and the older men eager for the warpath. Great Bull held up his hand.

'Listen to my words,' he said sternly. 'To ride against the Apache is an honour, but to defend the tepees of our women is as great an honour. Not all can go, for if they did then we would be defenceless against our enemies. So, the young men, the new warriors, will go so as to gain their first scalps, while the older braves will remain to protect the village. I have spoken.'

There was a little argument, but not much, for all accepted the reason and truth of his words. Grey Horse, bubbling with excitement, went to collect his weapons and horse, and Sam, equally excited, did likewise. He made a brief farewell to Red Cloud and Laughing Water and within minutes was ready for the journey.

His emotions as he rode with the band of other young braves, some twenty in all, were mixed. He was basically a white man with a veneer of Indian. He was excited at the prospect of action and glad to be with his friends, but that was as far as he thought. He did not think of the actual war, the killing and the danger of being killed. To him, as to the Indians, it was just an exciting game much the same as he had played a dozen times with the young boys in the past. The only real difference was that now he would use real weapons with real intent. In effect it was a further part of his training, and if he should be successful then he would be able to sit among the warriors and join in Council as the elders discussed the policy of the tribe.

Sam knew that this raid was going to give him the chance of becoming a real man.

5

Sam had been twelve when captured by the Sioux and he lived as an Indian for five years before taking the initiation ceremony as a warrior. During those five years the rumoured Civil War had flamed and torn the South to a shambles as Sherman marched through Georgia to the sea. The war had died and homeless Confederate troops, hungry for peace and a new life, had looked at their ruined economy and turned their faces westwards. The South was in the process of reorganization, freed slaves wandered in starving misery, exploited by the carpetbaggers and vote-catchers of the North. Once great houses were burned shells and the restless aftermath of war surged and strained at the new frontiers.

The true settlement of the West had begun.

Cochise knew it; knew, too, that the Indians of the plains were fighting a losing battle with the white man. Again and again he sent his warriors down into the desert to burn and pillage the wagon trains. Again and again the cavalry rode against him, harrying his braves and destroying his villages. The Mexicans too, smarting at old injuries, did their best to stamp out the Apache and reserved their particular hate for Cochise, the Scourge of the South, as they had named him.

And scourge he was.

The land of the Apache lay in hills and desert to the north of Mexico and across the route to southern California. Further north the Cheyenne merged with the Sioux, who in turn were followed by the Dakotas. The tribes lay down the Mid-West from the borders of Canada to the Rio Grande, and they all had one thing in common, they all hated the white invaders with a fanatical hatred. But hatred wasn't enough. Time and again small bands of warriors smashed and burned, only to be harried by the mounted cavalry of the Union Forces, their villages burned, their men and women forced into reservations. Most of these reservations were just simple death-traps, the Indians, taken from their plains and hills, could not live in the mosquito-infested swamp lands granted to them. They died of the coughing sickness, and the remainder, starving and desperate, broke out again and again to harry and pillage until the signing of a new treaty which, as before, was broken almost before the ink was dry.

The East was moving towards the West, and the Indians, small in number, could not be allowed to halt the march of progress.

All this had happened to the Seminoles, the Crow, the Blackfeet and other tribes to the east. Some had been driven back into the lands of their hereditary enemies, there to live on sufferance until, mad with hurt pride, they flung themselves away in futile war.

The warning was plain and Cochise knew what must inevitably happen to all the Indians of the plains. But he fought against it, fighting more to earn the respect of the invaders than with any real hope of winning a ceaseless war. He fought until the time was ripe to make a treaty, and then, when that treaty was broken, fought again. He had cut all communications between the east and west, harried the troops based in Apache Pass, and ruled as much as any man could rule, over the hills and deserts of the southern part of New Mexico.

Into this delicate balance Sam, riding with a mixed group of Sioux and Cheyenne, entered on the warpath.

The Cheyenne laughed and joked as they rode, for Indians, despite the opinion of the white man, had a highly developed sense of humour. They often played practical jokes on each other and acted to one another with the easy familiarity of brothers. The Sioux kept themselves a little apart from the

Cheyenne, for after all they were uneasy allies. For this raid they would fight and operate as one unit, but it was quite possible that, after the raid was over and the warriors returned to their own tepees, they would meet only to fight each other. So ingrained was the custom of warfare that it was almost impossible to unite any of the Indians into a unified whole. This lack of unity was their greatest weakness, that and the fact that to them a war was a mere raid done with and over and soon forgotten. Had they been able to unite themselves and accept discipline and the fact that a war did not stop after a raid, but went on and on until one side was utterly defeated, then the white man would never have been able to gain a new world so easily. The Indian, in this respect, was his own greatest enemy.

Sam didn't think of this as he rode. He gripped the sides of his pony, riding, as did all the Indians, bare-backed, and his eyes were eager as he searched the hills around them for some sign of the enemy. He was dressed in fine skin trousers, moccasins, and a string of beads supporting his medicine bag. At his waist hung scalping knife and tomahawk, across his shoulders hung his quiver and bow, and he cradled his rifle in his hands. As yet he wore no feathers, but he had painted his face and torso with a mixture of red and yellow ochre, one half of his body and face red, the other yellow. Grey Horse had evolved an elaborate pattern of colour for his personal use, for he, like most young braves, had gone to extremes in his warpaint. Most of the older warriors contented themselves with streaks of red and circles of yellow or black, but each could alter or change his paint as he wished, it had no religious significance and was only used to terrify the enemy.

Abruptly the Cheyenne fell silent as a scout, riding his horse with accustomed ease, came riding across the broken ground towards the war-party.

'Apache village three miles to the south,' he said. 'Two guards this side.'

Black Eagle nodded and gestured for five men to attend to the guards. He made the main party wait until they had reported back that the watching men were now in no position to give the alarm and, riding with silent caution, led the way towards the village.

There was no laughing or talking now. The war-party rode in grim silence, their eyes watchful as they stared about them, their hands tense as they gripped their weapons.

The trail led through underbrush and broken foothills, wending between time-worn stone and weathered boulders. The tension mounted as they approached the village, the scouts wriggling like snakes as they dropped from their ponies and advanced to spy the land. They returned, waved, and suddenly the entire party was galloping forward.

They shrieked as they rode, yelling their war-whoops, waving their rifles and shooting into the air. They thundered towards the wickiups of the Apache, their ponies' hooves thudding against the ground, and as they rode they sent a hail of death towards the few figures seen among the wickiups.

It was exciting. It was a game. It was living instead of routine. Sam screamed and yelled with the rest, firing his rifle at dimly-seen shapes and reloading as he rode. Beside him a screaming warrior coughed and toppled from his pony. Another screamed as a feathered shaft suddenly bristled in his chest, and a third groaned as a rifle bullet smashed in his skull. Then they were among the wood and hide wickiups and the fighting became hand-to-hand.

Grey Horse yelled as he drove his lance into the side of an Apache and, jumping from his horse, drew his scalping knife and took his trophy. Sam dodged a swung tomahawk, squeezed the trigger of his rifle and felt his face grow wet with the blood which sprayed towards him. All around him men yelled and women screamed as they fought and struggled, then, suddenly, it was over and Black Eagle was giving quick directions.

'Collect the horses,' he ordered. 'Collect the guns and blankets and make packs. Take what women you will, but leave the children. Kill the warriors and old men. Hurry.'

To the Indians it was an old game. Swiftly they went from wickiup to wickiup, collecting blankets, rifles, food, leatherwork and other booty. Personal belongings such as weapons other than rifles or scalps they did not take. They moved fast and efficiently and, almost before Sam knew it, they were ready to leave.

'A good raid,' said Grey Horse importantly. His body was streaked with blood and at his belt hung a fresh scalp. He looked at Sam.

'Waugh! You seem to have bathed in blood. Yet you have no scalp to hang in your tepee?'

'No.' Sam felt a strange reluctance to collect scalps. It was hard to explain, for there was no real reason against it. The removal of a scalp from a dead enemy was a proof of valour and a prized decoration. A patch of hair and skin about three inches across was removed from the crown of the head of an enemy. In itself scalping was not fatal. Many white men were alive who had been knocked unconscious and scalped, only to regain their senses after the raid. Such men had a peculiar lost expression, the result of the cutting of the muscles supporting the facial structure, and though after a while the expression vanished, yet they remained self-conscious of their scarred heads.

'You are weak,' said Grey Horse. 'To collect scalps is a mark of the Sioux. Your wife will think little of you if you have no scalps for your tepee.'

'I am not weak,' said Sam tightly. 'To mar the dead is the act of a coward.'

'You call me so?' Anger narrowed Grey Horse's eyes. 'You doubt my courage?'

'Less talk,' snapped Black Eagle. 'The Apache are not women that they will forget this wrong we have done them. They will ride after us and recover what we have taken. Ride!'

'We will discuss this matter later,' said Grey Horse. 'No man calls me coward to my face.'

'I called you no coward,' said Sam. 'I do not wish to mar the dead, you called me weak because of that. Am I to swallow your words?'

Grey Horse shrugged and rode forward, Sam following close behind. He had reached a clump of bushes when Sam saw the gleam of a rifle barrel pointing towards his companion. Instinctively he rode forward, pushing Grey Horse to one side just as a bullet whined through the space where he had been. The young brave recovered his balance, threw up his rifle and fired into the bushes.

Immediately they were fighting for their lives.

A band of Apache broke from the bushes and charged towards the war-party. They yelled once and then fell silent as tomahawks flashed and arrows thrummed. Sam yelled, threw up his rifle and knocked aside a tomahawk which threatened to split his skull, then as his pony reared and went down, rolled clear to find himself standing beside Grey Horse.

'We fight together,' said the warrior. 'You shall see if I am a coward.'

'Save your breath for the fighting,' snapped Sam. 'This is a trap and we'll be lucky to escape alive.'

He grunted as a wave of painted warriors came towards him.

It was a blind mêlée of painted bodies and swift, savage action. A lance drove towards his chest and he dodged, barely in time to avoid the sharp point. A tomahawk swung towards his head, he ducked, stabbed upwards with his knife and felt his hand and arm grow wet with blood. A choked cry from Grey Horse made him turn, and Sam stepped forward as a brave stooped over the fallen figure of the young warrior. Sam wasted no time, he stabbed, twisted and saw stars as something thudded against his skull. Groggily he shook his head and, straddling the prostrate figure of Grey Horse, readied himself for death.

It never came.

A call echoed from the edge of the clearing around the village, a sharp, peremptory call, and as suddenly as the fighting had begun, it was over. Black Eagle and the Cheyenne together with the Sioux were herded together by a ring of Apache, and Sam, his head throbbing from the blow it had received, found himself standing beside Grey Horse facing the threatening circle of braves.

'They are going to kill us,' said Grey Horse. His face was impassive, but his eyes reflected his pain. He had been stabbed in the side and blood made a thin trickle over his bronzed skin. Sam examined the wound, satisfied himself that it was not serious, and straightened as a man came riding towards the village.

He was a tall, proud Indian, his face heavy and sombre with thought. He carried a rifle and a knife hung at his waist. He wore no paint and his long, black hair was held by a thong of rawhide. He dismounted and stepped forward, then stood and surveyed the captives.

'I am Cochise,' he said abruptly. 'Who leads you?'

'I am Black Eagle. I lead them.' Black Eagle stared defiantly at the noted Indian chief. 'For long and long have my people suffered from the hands of the Apache. For many moons we have seen our horses and our women carried off by your braves. So we are here to take back what is ours.'

'But you are not all of the Cheyenne.' Cochise stared at the Sioux warriors, each with the typical crest of hair on their shaven heads. 'What quarrel have I with the Sioux?'

'No quarrel,' admitted Black Eagle. 'We called to them as brothers and, as brothers, they answered our call. These young warriors rode with the Cheyenne for the sake of scalps and plunder. Is that so wrong?'

'To be a brother to each cannot be wrong,' said Cochise. He stared at Black Eagle. 'You are my prisoner and if I wish you will die. You have done my people great wrong and such wrong should not go unpunished. You know that?'

'Are we children to be frightened of words?' Black Eagle stared his scorn. 'We are yours to do with as you wish. Kill us if that is your will.'

'It is not my will.' Cochise handed his rifle to a warrior and addressed the prisoners.

'Listen to me men of the Cheyenne. Listen to me men of the Sioux. You have done my people much wrong and it would be right should you suffer for that wrong. Many moons ago you would have so suffered, but things have happened since the old days and the ways of our fathers are not the ways we can still follow. We are brothers, we the

Apache, the Cheyenne, the Sioux, the Dakotas. We of the plains and we of the hills and deserts, we are brothers. We are the Indians and we are brothers. Is this not so?'

'It is so,' said Black Eagle. 'My brother talks with a straight tongue.'

'Among us have come those whose skins are not of our colour. The white men have come into our lands and they are stealing our lands from us and we can do nothing. They give us papers and say that such and such will happen and it is not so. The white men and the long knives are taking from us that which is ours and that which was our fathers before us. Is this not so?'

'It is so,' admitted Black Eagle.

'To the south the Mexicans are now paying much money for the scalp of an Apache. To the east the white men have herded our brothers of the Crow, the Blackfeet, the Seminole, and put them into reservations in which they die. This, too, is happening here. I speak the truth.'

'We hear your words,' said Black Eagle.

'When brother fights brother it is bad. When brother fights brother and lets the wolf steal his papoose from his cradle it is worse. When brother fights brother and his tepee is stolen from him, his women taken, his horses killed, that is even worse. Are my words reaching your hearts?'

The analogy was too plain to miss. From the assembled warriors, prisoners and captors alike, came a deep guttural sound of assent. Cochise heard it, waited for it to die, then lifted his arm for silence.

'I speak of what is true words, as you all know. You are my brothers and we are all fighting the white man. I say to you that it is a bad thing for brother to fight brother at this time. It must not be, for if we so fight then we lose all.' He stepped forward a little more and stared at Black Eagle. 'To ride the warpath and wage war, tribe to tribe, is a good thing, for how else can the warriors reach manhood? To steal horses and capture women is a good thing, for how else can a man strengthen his tribe? All the ways of our fathers are good ways. So we have lived for many, many years. But so can we live no longer.'

Again the deep, guttural sound.

'This I say to you,' said Cochise. 'Let us bury the hatchet and smoke the pipe of peace. Let your people and mine live in peace one with the other until the white man has been defeated and these lands are ours once again. This I say to you. What say you?'

'I agree!' Black Eagle stared at the other prisoners. 'I speak for Cheyenne. We will smoke the pipe of peace and there will be no war between us.'

'It is good. What say the Sioux?'

'I agree!' Sam stepped forward. 'I will not fight the Apache.'

'Do you speak for all?'

'No. Great Bull is my chief and for him I cannot speak. But send a messenger with your words and he will

107

listen to them. Great Bull is a wise man and will tell the straight tongue from the forked tongue. Send a messenger to the tepees of the Sioux and tell him what you have told us.'

'Let each speak as his heart,' said Cochise. 'When all is ready we will bury the hatchet and smoke the pipe of peace.'

All agreed, not through fear of death should they refuse, for they thought nothing of death, but because the words of the Apache chief had kindled their hearts. Even Sam felt himself hate the white man, and he realized how foolish it was for the Indians to fight each other in the face of a common enemy. He watched as a tomahawk was buried in the ground and the dirt smoothed over the place.

'As this hatchet is buried so we bury our hate and fear,' said Cochise, and Black Eagle repeated it after him. The pipe of peace, a long-stemmed instrument made of carved stone, was filled, lit, and passed from man to man. Each took a puff before passing it on and then, surprisingly, it was over. The Apache took back the things which had been stolen, returned their prisoners' horses, and that was that.

Sam was very thoughtful as they rode back the way they had come. The ceremony of the buried hatchet did not surprise him, nor did the passing of the peace pipe. He knew that no one would molest them now and that the Cheyenne and Apache would not fight until due warning had been given, the hatchet dug up again, and a ceremonial declaration of enmity made. Until then no member of either tribe would attack the other. While they would not necessarily work or fight together, they would be neutral towards each other. The word of an Indian was his pride and no one would break it. Both Cheyenne and the Sioux who had ridden with them were honour bound to observe the oath they had taken and no one would think anything the worse for them doing so. Indeed, should they break their word then they would be ostracized and expelled from the tribe, for the honour of the tribe depended on the honour of every individual.

'How is your wound?' Sam asked after a while to Grey Horse, who rode at his side. 'Does it give you pain?'

'It is nothing.'

'Cochise is a mighty warrior,' said Sam reflectively. 'Is it true that he has beaten the white men back almost to the sea?'

'Who knows?' Grey Horse shifted on his pony's back. 'For many years Cochise has fought the Mexicans and then the whites. He has fought the long knives and made the hills safe for the Apache. He is a great warrior.'

Sam nodded. He had heard the gossip about the Apache chief and knew that he had won several victories over the cavalry, the 'long knives', so called by the Indians because of the sabres they carried.

'He looks a leader of men,' he said admiringly. 'He talks peace with the

Indian and talks war against the white invaders. Will he win the war with the soldiers?'

'Many things are possible,' said Grey Horse. 'He will fight and he will win if he wishes it.'

Sam shrugged. Whilst almost an Indian he couldn't really believe in the possibility of any tribe or group of tribes ever beating the white men. He had dim memories of his own home, the troubled area of Kentucky, and knew that should even a small percentage of the men who lived there decide to move West, then the Indians would be swamped by sheer weight of numbers. His mind told him that, but his training, the veneer which had made him an Indian warrior, refused to accept the fact that the Indian way of life was drawing to a close.

The journey was made in silence, with none of the laughing and joking which had lightened the outward trip. The warriors, while not exactly ashamed, had no cause for rejoicing, for they had lost several of their number and had nothing to show for their trouble. Black Eagle, after visiting his village, announced his intention of carrying the words of Cochise to Great Bull, and after resting for a day the Sioux and the Cheyenne chief continued northward.

Grey Horse's wound healed without complication, though he was stiff and a little weak from loss of blood. Sam had bound it with a poultice made from crushed leaves, and the young warrior was able to keep up the fast pace set by the others. By the time they arrived near the village he had recovered his good spirits and was very proud of himself. He spoke to Sam on the last camp of their journey before reaching the village.

'Tomorrow we will return and I shall make a coup stick and ornament it with feathers to tell of the raid.' He looked thoughtful. 'I shall wear a feather in my hair as befits one who has taken his first scalp.'

'The Apache took the scalp from

you,' reminded Sam.

'It does not matter. I took it and will wear the feather.'

'True, but what will you tell the women when they ask to see the scalp of which you boast?'

'I shall tell them that — ' Grey Horse paused. 'I see what you mean. They would laugh at me for losing it as soon as it was taken.'

'Yes.'

'And yet we fought well. I have the marks of battle on my body.'

'Let the scar of your wound speak for itself, Grey Horse,' said Sam with a wisdom beyond his years. 'A silent tongue and a scar mean more than a loud voice and an unmarked skin to those with eyes to see. Let the wind whisper of your deeds while you remain silent.'

'Your words are wise,' said Grey Horse. He looked thoughtful. 'You are a white man, Stone Face. Is that not true?'

'I am a Sioux.'

'You are a Sioux,' agreed the young warrior. 'But you are not like us in many ways. Red Cloud and Laughing Water are your parents by choice, not by nature. Is this not so?'

'And if it is?'

'You are my brother,' said Grey Horse evenly. 'You are my brother as though you had been born in the tepees of my people. Yet it comes to me that you are closer to me than any brother. You stood over me when I lay wounded and you fought to save my life.'

'It was nothing.'

'It was the act of a brother,' said Grey Horse. He hesitated again. 'Stone Face, I would be your brother in blood. I would be that you and I are one for all time and in all things. Will you be my *ananda*.'

'Your *ananda*?'

'Even so.' Grey Horse glanced up at the sky. 'It comes to me that there are strange things walking the land and the spirits whisper to my soul that all is not well with our people. I would be of you

114

and with you so that your strength shall be my strength, my strength your strength and we shall be together in all things.' He held out his left wrist. 'Give me your blood — brother.'

Sam, took a deep breath and held out his left arm. It was a ceremony familiar enough and yet at the same time rare. For an Indian to offer himself as a blood-brother was for him to give himself body and soul to his opposite partner. The ties of blood were stronger by far than those of nature. A man chose his blood-brother while his natural brothers were chosen for him. It was not a thing to be taken lightly.

Grey Horse slipped his knife from his belt and slit the skin on the back of his left wrist. Quickly he did the same to the arm Sam held out to him, and then dropping the knife he pressed his wound against that in Sam's arm, holding the limb tight so that the blood mingled.

'My blood in your body,' he intoned seriously. 'Your blood in my body. You are as myself and I am you. If you are cold then I shall shiver, if hot then I burn. If you hunger I shall grow faint, and if you laugh I shall be happy. Where you go there also I go, when you die then I die with you. One body, one spirit, one soul. We are closer than brothers of the flesh, we are brothers of the blood. Call and I shall answer. My *ananda*, my blood-brother, my life.'

It was a simple thing, a primitive thing, but it was sincere, and as Sam rubbed the cut on his arm he felt a strange elation. He was an Indian now more than ever. He was blood-brother to Grey Horse of the Sioux.

He was smiling as he settled down for sleep.

6

Stone Face stepped from his tepee and stared up at the morning sun. He stretched, feeling the last lassitude of sleep slip from him as he breathed the clear spring air. Around him the village was stirring into life, women were stooped over the cooking fire and children ran with shrill cries as they dodged between the skin tents. Men, old men and young, sat and blinked and rubbed grease into their arms to strengthen their muscles. Warriors tested their bows or worked at their winter tasks of chipping heads for their arrows. The old squaws sat and chewed hides to render them soft and smooth and as supple as silk.

Three times had Ghost Face held the land in his iron grip since the night when Grey Horse had taken Sam to be his red brother. The two boys had grown into men and both bore the pale scars of many wounds. Their fighting had been confined to tribal conflicts with the Dakotas and the Cheyenne, though since Sam had almost been shot by a white scout he had surprised, and Grey Horse had lain near death after being beaten by some prospectors. But these were isolated incidents, and on the whole the past three years had been uneventful.

Sam breathed deeply again then smiled as Grey Horse came towards him. The warrior looked despondent and Sam guessed that his courtship was not proceeding as the young man would wish. He called to his friend as he stepped forward.

'Grey Horse, have the spirits taken your smile?'

'I am sad, Stone Face.'

'The father of Many Smiles does not look upon Grey Horse with approval?'

'Heavy Grass is a greedy old man,' said Grey Horse disrespectfully. 'He knows that Many Smiles desires to be my squaw and he knows that I am a good warrior and would provide much food for her. Yet he refuses to give me her in marriage!'

'Heavy Grass perhaps desires many rich gifts,' said Sam shrewdly. 'Broken Arrow also desires the maid and, so I have heard, has offered many horses for her.'

'Broken Arrow is an old man,' snapped Grey Horse. 'Yet you are right. Today will Heavy Grass choose. Broken Arrow and myself must appear with our gifts before his tepee when the sun is high. Then he will give Many Smiles to the man he chooses.' Grey Horse kicked at the ground. 'Waugh! It is enough to make a man doubt the spirits!'

'Come and watch the contests,' said Sam cheerfully. 'The young boys are at their games and the sight may remind you of the days when you were young and knew not worry. Come, let us watch the new warriors of the Sioux.'

Sullenly Grey Horse allowed Sam to

lead him from the village and towards the place where the contests were held.

The contests were held in a small valley outside the village, and when Sam and Grey Horse arrived ten boys were standing in line. Walking Dog, the shaman, was talking to them in his deep voice. In his hand he held a small water skin.

'I will give each of you a mouthful of water,' he said. 'You are not to swallow it. You must hold it in your mouths while you run for two miles.'

The ten boys, all young and all dwarfed by the tall shaman, nodded eagerly and each took his mouthful of water. Then at a signal from the shaman they raced off. Sam watched them as they ran to a stunted tree and then chased back again. They ran very fast and were back in just over ten minutes. They lined up and the shaman walked along the line, and as he passed each boy spat his mouthful of water on the ground. All but one boy had managed to retain his water.

'What happened to you?' demanded Walking Dog of the unfortunate boy.

'I stumbled,' said the boy miserably. 'I almost fell and I swallowed my water.'

'Your tepee.'

The boy turned away without protest. His father, who was sitting with some other men watching the contests, rose and went with him. Both were much ashamed.

A warrior called Twisted Feather glanced at Sam and traced a pattern idly in the dirt. 'I have a son,' he said casually. 'I think he is a good boy.'

'I have no son,' said Sam.

'Nor I,' said Grey Horse.

'He is a good boy,' insisted Twisted Feather.

'I have no son,' repeated Sam, then glanced at a lad he knew to be the son of Bare Mountain, a warrior who was lying sick with a broken leg. 'I have no son, but I think that the son of Bare Mountain is a good boy.'

'I have a horse,' said Twisted Feather. 'A paint.'

'I have a horse also,' said Sam. 'A black.'

'It is well,' said Twisted Feather. 'Let them fight.'

The two boys who had listened to the conversation and the bet faced each other and began to wrestle. They wrapped their wiry arms around each other and tried to throw each other to the ground. All sat and watched them silently and, as they struggled, other bets were made among the warriors, each man backing one of the boys with a rifle, bow, blanket or, in extreme cases, with a pony.

The son of Twisted Feather suddenly grabbed the other boy's wrist and twisted his arm around his back. Exerting pressure he began to bear upwards on the trapped arm. The son of Bare Mountain bit his lips but said nothing. The other boy raised the arm still further, and his opponent bit his lips until the blood ran over his chin to keep himself from crying 'enough', the signal which would have stopped the bout. The boy kept up the leverage until the son of Bare Mountain felt that his arm would break, then swiftly he managed to twist around and catch the other boy under the leg with his free arm. Lifting him he threw him down and caused him to release his grip, and before he could recover had jumped on him, his knee digging into the groin as he got a headlock on the other boy. Grimly the son of Bare Mountain applied pressure until the face of his opponent began to turn red and his eyes began to bulge.

The watching men made no move to interfere.

The son of Bare Mountain continued to apply the pressure. The other boy suddenly relaxed, but still he squeezed. Then the boy fainted, his head rolling loosely on his shoulders. Walking Dog rose from where he had been sitting and threw water on the unconscious boy's face.

'He was brave,' said Sam. 'He did not give up.'

'Yes,' said Twisted Feather proudly. 'I will bring you the horse.'

'No,' said Sam. 'Your son was brave. I do not win the horse. He could have done no more to win than what he did.' He moved away before Twisted Feather could argue.

Walking Dog next gave the boys small bows and arrows and divided them into two teams, five a side. He separated them and made them stand facing each other at a distance of about twenty-five yards.

'This will make you quick,' he said. 'You will shoot at each other until all your arrows are gone.'

The boys began shooting at each other with the small bows. The arrows had blunt heads and could not kill, but they could give a nasty bruise. One of the boys was hit just above the eye and his face was covered with blood. He did not run away, but continued shooting until another arrow hit him in the stomach and doubled him up. Walking Dog watched until all the arrows had been shot and collected, then made the boys run a foot race over stony ground.

'Remember your youth, Grey Horse?' Sam smiled at the eager youngsters as they obeyed the shaman, knowing that all their instruction had a purpose and would be valuable in later life.

'I could wish that I were young again,' said the warrior. 'See, the sun mounts and soon I must be at the tepee of Heavy Grass. I have few horses and few blankets. With the peace between us and the Apache and the Cheyenne not wanting war, there has been little chance for plunder. It was not so in my father's time.'

'Have a good heart, brother,' said Sam. 'If gifts will win the maiden for you, then she will be yours.'

'If she is not mine then I think I will ride from the village and not return,' said Grey Horse gloomily. He glanced at the sun. 'Wish me well, brother, I go to meet my fate.'

Sam smiled as he stared after the young warrior. Grey Horse was of an age to be married, even though Sam himself was the older by two years, yet he had no destre to take an Indian wife and settle down in his own tepee. Instead, he resolved to give Grey Horse a surprise, and returning to the village he collected some things and made his way to the tent of Heavy Grass.

He arrived just as the old man was judging the two men who desired his daughter in marriage. Broken Arrow had arrived with three horses and some fine goods. Grey Horse with but two ponies and very little else. Heavy Grass examined the goods, rubbed his chin and seemed about to speak.

'A moment!' Sam stepped forward leading two ponies and carrying a rifle. 'Before you say what is in your heart, Heavy Grass, may I add my gifts to those of my brother?' Sam smiled at the discomforted Broken Arrow. 'Discord in a tepee.' he said, 'is not worth the hair of a horse's mane. Young wives are bought dearly when they give a man no peace. Many Smiles desires my brother

Grey Horse as her warrior. I give what I can to my brother so that Heavy Grass will give Grey Horse his daughter.'

'Heavy Grass was about to give Many Smiles to Grey Horse,' lied the old man. 'Your gifts, though welcome, do not cause me to favour Grey Horse.'

'I thank you for this, Stone Face,' said Grey Horse sincerely. He, like all the others watching, knew that the extra gifts had won him the girl. Not that Heavy Grass was being greedy, his task as a father was to find the best warrior he could for his daughter, and when it came to a choice between two or more suitors, it was only human nature for him to pick the one with the most gifts. He was losing the labour of his daughter and thus deserved recompense. Most Indian fathers usually left the actual selecting of a husband for their daughters to their wives, so that the actual buying of a wife was really similar to a white man buying his betrothed an engagement ring. The Indians, however, far more practical in their everyday dealings, were interested in horses and goods of use, if not of high intrinsic value. They had a saying for such cases. Food in the stomach is worth more than sighs in the wind. The warrior who could bring back plenty of game for his squaw was valued more than a romantic type who would let his family suffer.

The marriage ceremony was as simple as most things connected with the Indian tribal life. Less important than the initiation ceremony, it was not regarded as in any way permanent and no great oaths were sworn on either side. Walking Dog, dressed in robes, stood before a fire and asked the simple, routine questions of the couple.

'Grey Horse, you have looked on this woman with the eyes of love and wish to take her into your tepee. This you will do, and care for her and her children with all your heart, your strength, your spirit. Say you so?'

'So I say.'

'Many Smiles, you have looked with

eyes of love on Grey Horse and he has given your father many gifts so that you may come and live with him in his tepee. You will care for him and cook his food. You will love his children and think of him in all things. Say you so?'

'So I say.'

'It is well.' Walking Dog tied a strip of rawhide around their wrists, tying their hands together. He stooped and picked up a handful of soil which he scattered over them. He picked a brand from the fire and waved it over their heads. He took a piece of bread and broke it and gave each a piece.

'With earth, fire and food I bless this union. Go now and be as one.' And that was all.

Grey Horse led his bride to where their horses were waiting and together, the young couple rode off into the underbrush. They would stay alone together for a whole month, during which time none would speak to them. Many Smiles had gathered together food and blankets and had built a small tent deep in the undergrowth. There the couple would stay, living in close harmony so that they would get to know each other. It was the custom.

Sam sighed as he watched them ride away. He knew that he would miss his friend, and for a moment wondered why he hadn't married one of the young women who had often hinted that his advances would be looked on with favour should he ask for their hands in marriage. Indian boys and girls matured young and were married young. There was nothing strange in a boy taking his initiation at fifteen, riding the warpath at sixteen, and being a father a year later. The economy of the tribe made early marriage essential, for a man alone could not take a full part in the communal life. Also the young girls wanted to leave the tepees of their parents and enter a full life. A married woman had many privileges denied to a single girl; she was allowed to wander at will, and her husband, if he was a good warrior, could provide her with many luxuries.

But the main incentive to early marriage was the constant necessity to replace the old blood with new.

Warfare, hard living, the nomadic way of life all helped to keep down the numbers of the plains Indians. Not at any time had there been more than half a million Indians in the entire Mid-West, and their numbers were steadily decreasing owing to their losses in fighting the white man. Each warrior who died weakened the tribe by just that amount. A sharp battle would leave many empty tepees and so, in order to keep the tribes at full strength, early marriages and many children were desirable. The increase would have been far greater if it had not been for the religious ruling which prevented an Indian woman from having more than one child every three years. For the first three years of a child's life it was carried in a cradle, its limbs massaged regularly and its every want supplied. This system, instead of weakening the baby, actually strengthened it and it was owing to this system in early childhood that the Indians had such a straight, proud posture. Everything was sublimated to the demands of the new-born child. Every want was supplied and every wish granted. It made for a wonderful sense of security, but, unlike the white men, it did not make for a large increase in population.

Sam felt a little lost as Grey Horse and Many Smiles rode away. He felt restless, burning with the need for action, and strode through the village hoping that something would occur so that he could be on the move. He knew that he could mount his pony and go riding if he wished. He could even make a lone raid on the Dakotas, or go riding down to the trading post the prospectors had set up about fifty miles to the east. Sam didn't much care for the trading post, his white blood was too strong and he didn't like the sneers and gibes of the bearded men who lounged around the store. Also, the trader often cheated the Indians and Sam had done much to stop the selling of the raw spirit which had so rotted the moral fibre of so many warriors.

He was walking past the big Council tepee when Great Bull called to him.

'Stone Face, a word with you.'

'Yes, Great Bull?' Sam stepped within the tepee and glanced curiously at a brave lying on a blanket. He was a thin warrior, a brave of the Dakotas, his paint smeared and a red-splotched wound on his left side. Great Bull's wife was tending him, washing the wound and preparing a poultice of crushed leaves to bind over the gash. Walking Dog, his seamed old face betraying his seriousness, squatted before the fire.

'This man rode into the village at dawn,' said Great Bull without hesitation. 'He is of our enemies and was wounded. He took a risk in coming to us, but he carries heavy words and he will not be harmed. His words must be told to every warrior. I would that you would listen to his words and give your council.'

Sam flushed a little and joined Walking Dog before the fire. It was a great honour to be asked to sit in Council, an honour usually reserved for the elders of the tribe. He stared at the wounded Indian as the man began to speak.

'Many moons ago we were at war with the white man,' said the brave. 'Sitting Bull was our chief then as he is now, and he is a great and wise chief. Many warriors were slain and many widows wailed to the dead. Food was short, and during the time of the great cold many died. They were bad times for the Dakotas.'

'It was a bad time,' agreed Great Bull. 'Continue.'

'After many wars the white soldiers came and they gave us a paper. On this paper they had trapped the land and they said that such and such was for the Dakota and that none would enter or try to take it away for ever and ever. This paper Sitting Bull called a treaty, it was the white man's promise that if there would be no more war we should not be harmed and could live in peace on the land our fathers had hunted, Many grumbled at this giving up of our land, but as Sitting Bull said, this land is big and there is room for all. Many blankets and rifles, sacks of flour and horses were given to the Dakotas as gifts from the white man. We washed off our warpaint and buried the hatchet and lived at peace. We trusted the word of the long knives.'

'The long knives speak with a forked tongue,' said Great Bull. 'Their word is of the air and their promises as nothing. Did not Sitting Bull know this?'

'He knew, but we were weary of war and our children were starving. Winter drew near and we could not fight and not gather food. He decided to trust the long knives.' The wounded man spat. 'Waugh! We were as children.'

'Speak on,' said Walking Dog quietly. The old shaman glanced at Sam. 'We listen.'

'For a while we lived in peace. Then we gathered for the buffalo hunt and rode out to collect food for the winter. There were few buffalo, less buffalo than the oldest man alive remembered. Food was short that winter.'

'Speak on,' said Sam sharply. The Sioux, like the Dakotas and the Cheyenne and, to a lesser extent the Apache, depended on the buffalo as their main source of food and supplies. The beasts provided everything the Indians needed. Their hides made the tepees, their sinews the bowstrings, their bones the fuel and arrowheads. The flesh was cut into strips and dried, the fat rendered down so as to grease hair and waterproof garments. Nothing of the buffalo was wasted and the entire economy of the tribe depended on a constant supply of the huge animals. Twice a year all the warriors would ride out and kill as many of the beasts as they could. The women would prepare the meat for use during the Fall and winter, and during the cold weather both men and women would work at the hides and bones, making weapons and clothing, new tepees and warm coverings. In the old days the buffalo herds had been so thick that they had shaken the ground as they moved over the prairie, but of recent years the huge herds were getting smaller and smaller.

'In the spring we rode out again for buffalo. It was not a good thing to do, for the buffalo hunt is at the end of the year when the calves have been born and the herds replenished. We rode for many days and then we heard the sound of many guns. We rode closer and found that many white men were shooting the buffalo. They had new guns and they killed and killed and killed until the ground was hidden by the bodies. We watched. They skinned the buffalo and left the meat to rot. We followed. They were interested only in the skins. They had killed more buffalo than would be needed to provide food for all the Dakotas for one winter, and they had killed them all in one day.'

'And then?'

'We attacked the white men. We rode against them and killed them all, but many were lost in the fighting and I was wounded.'

'So why came you here?'

'I have done a bad thing. I have broken the peace by killing the white man. Sitting Bull will be angry, but that is not why I came. What has happened to the Dakotas can happen to the Sioux. If there are no more buffalo then we die. The white men must stop killing the buffalo.'

And that was that.

It was so simple as to allow of no argument. If the buffalo died then the Indians would have no food and would die. The white men who had killed the buffalo were, in effect, killing the Indians by indirect methods. Sam could appreciate the hate and fury of the warriors who had seen the wanton slaughter.

Great Bull looked thoughtful as the injured warrior ceased talking. He sat for a long moment staring into the fire, and then lifting his head he stared at Sam.

'Stone Face, what say you?'

'We must protect the buffalo,' said Sam immediately. 'We must send out parties to drive away the men who kill for the love of killing. This we must do and do at once or there will be no buffalo to feed us this winter. They are my words.'

'They are good words,' said Walking Dog. 'They are direct and to the point, but look a little deeper, Stone Face, and think of this. If we guard the herds then there will be trouble with the white man. The long knives will come with many guns and they will protect the white men. There will be war and fighting and many warriors will be slain. How say you to this?'

'Are we children to run from trouble? Should we sit and listen to the cries of hungry children? For too long have the white men robbed and stolen from the Indian. They despise us and call us savages and shoot us like the dogs they call us. Now they take the food from our mouths and yet we do nothing. I say that we ride and protect the herds.'

'You speak well, Stone Face,' said Great Bull gently. 'You speak from your heart, but your heart is not the heart of an Indian. You say ride and protect the herds, which is good, but for how long must we do this?'

'For as long as the white men come to steal our food. For always if necessary.'

'That is a long time. Our young men will grow impatient and wander from their posts.'

'I would not desert,' said Sam, hotly. 'I would stay and wait and kill until the buffalo were left in peace.'

'Yes,' said Walking Dog quietly. 'You would. But you are a white man and not an Indian.'

'You lie!' Sam was flaming with rage. 'I am a Sioux!'

'Take not offence at an old man's words,' said Walking Dog. 'Listen to what I say then you will have understanding.' He sighed and settled himself more comfortably before the fire. 'You were old when you came to us, too old, but we allowed you to live, for Red Cloud wanted a son and his squaw was barren. You have grown into manhood and are a fine warrior, but you are not an Indian. You ride like a Sioux, you talk like one, eat like one, follow our ways as if you had been born in a tepee, but you are not a Sioux.

'You talk of guarding the herds and it is good talk, but it cannot be done. Our young men will not stay long in one place. They will not follow the buffalo and wait for an enemy which may not come. Indians ride and fight and ride again. So they have always done and so they will still do. Cochise, the Scourge of the South, has tried to do what you speak of. He is trying to make all the Apache obey one voice. He is doing something no Indian has ever done before, but he is a great warrior, Apache born, and yet even with the love they have for him his people still grumble at his words. Sitting Bull and Crazy Horse of the Dakotas are trying to unite their tribes so that the warriors will obey. It is a hard thing to do. For a white man it is a hard thing to understand. The Indian loves freedom, his own freedom, and will die rather than do what he does not wish to do.'

'So you think that I am not an Indian?'

'You are one of us, our own son, our own brother, but you think with the thoughts of a white man. This is so and this is what can never be different.' Walking Dog shrugged. 'It is what it is.'

Sam sighed, recognizing the fatalism of the Indian. The shaman was right. Sam's restlessness, his impatience, his eagerness for action stemmed from his early childhood. He was still basically a white man and though he could ride against them and even war with them, he could not immerse himself wholly in the timeless fatalism of the Indians. He had the same restless urge which even now was forcing the settlers to the West. Sam, despite his Indian training, could not forget his heritage.

Walking Dog smiled and rested his hand on Sam's arm.

'Be of good heart, Stone Face. You are of us and will stay with us. I spoke to show you that all is not as simple as you would think.'

'No.' Sam frowned in deep thought. 'Tell me,' he said suddenly, 'have you thought of this before?'

'Yes.'

'Is that why you have not sent me riding against the white men?'

'It is. It is hard for a man to forget his own. You are of the white men and yet you are of the Sioux. It would not be a good thing for you to kill your own!'

'I am a man,' said Sam tightly. 'A warrior of the Sioux. I am a brave and no man has the right to tell me what to do.' He rose. 'There are other braves who will join me. I am going to ride out and see if this man has spoken with a straight tongue. If I find the buffalo are being slaughtered I shall attack. I have spoken.'

'You may go,' said Great Bull wearily. 'You may take those who will ride with you. You will see what you see and send back word. I cannot stop you nor would I if I could.' He stared at Walking Dog. 'Tonight we sit in full Council. It comes to me that soon many widows will mourn the passing of their warriors. Waugh! If it will be then let it come. Can we defy the Gods?'

His words were brave but his face, as he stared into the fire, was sad with hidden thoughts.

7

Big Jim Ratford stood at the bar of a saloon in Homeville and washed the dust of travel from his throat with a generous swig of raw whiskey. He had changed little since the time when he had galloped madly from the scene of carnage with the boy following him. Big Jim didn't like to think of the boy and what must have happened. Fear rode with him as he galloped away and still sometimes he woke to the shuddering memory of the Indian war-whoops, the thud of hooves and the sickening knowledge that, if his horse floundered, he would die horribly.

After the incident he had returned to Fort Henry, there to be swept up in the tide of war. For a while he had acted as an Indian scout, later still he had ridden with the Union Forces based in New Mexico and, finally, had drifted back to his old stamping grounds. Now, dry after long travel, he stood and drank and let his eyes drift over the crowd thronging the saloon.

They were the usual bunch of men to be found on the frontier, hard, tough, dressed in leather or skin, some in the thick homespun of the settlers, but most of them wearing the garb of prospectors. Most of them were armed with the six-chambered Colt revolvers and cartridge belts now general in the West, and the majority also carried the curved knives known after the man who had designed them. Big Jim shifted his own revolver and bowie into a more comfortable position, then tensed as a man approached him.

'Have a drink, stranger?'

'Why not?' Big Jim waited as the bartender placed the bottle on the counter, poured out a glass of the raw spirit and drank it without taking his eyes off the man who had accosted him. The stranger, too, stared with frank interest.

He wore skins fringed and beaded in the Indian fashion, but he was not an Indian. He wore his hair long and sported a goatee beard and a heavy moustache. He wore two guns and a knife and his face was weathered to the colour of old oak.

'My name is Bullen,' he said. 'Wade Bullen. I know who you are.'

'Someone been talking?'

'The commander. I asked for a likely man to help me in a project I have in mind and he mentioned you. He said that you'd had experience of the country around here. Is that right?'

'Some. I used to boss the wagon trains heading west.'

'Then?'

'The war.' Big Jim scratched at his beard. 'What's on your mind, Wade?'

'Business.' Bullen stared about him and then jerked his head towards the door. 'Come up to my room in the hotel. I've a proposition which may interest you.'

'And if it doesn't?'

'Then maybe you can sell me some advice.' Bullen grinned and picked up the bottle, paying for it with a handful of silver dollars. 'Come on, Jim, what have you got to lose?'

Big Jim hesitated for a moment then shrugged. As the stranger had said, he had nothing to lose and, in fact, everything to gain. Big Jim had arrived in Homeville from his last prospecting tour utterly broke and had been thinking of trying to get a grubstake when Bullen had accosted him. Silently he followed the other up to his room in the single hotel the new-built township owned and sat down as he waited for the other man to speak.

'I'll put it plain, Jim,' said Wade. 'I'm representing a big Eastern syndicate and there's money for all who get in on the ground floor. I'd like for you to join me.'

'Prospecting?'

'No.' Wade looked curiously at the big man. 'Is that what you've been doing?'

'Yes. I took a turn through the hills looking for paydirt. I didn't find any.'

'Maybe there's none to find.'

'There's gold out there right enough. I've seen some nuggets and panned a river for a little dust. It's the main seam I'm looking for. Find it and I'll retire rich.'

'That's what you say.' Wade poured out more drinks. 'I've seen you prospectors before, you spend your lives looking for the yellow stuff and when you find it, if you do, you let yourselves get robbed by some high-pressure operator. Mostly you scratch around on a grub stake and get yourself killed by the Indians. I've got a better proposition than that.'

'I'm waiting to hear it. Trading?'

'No. Trading is all right but it's small returns.' Wade leaned forward. 'What do you know about buffalo?'

'Buffalo?'

'That's right. Buffalo. What do you know about them?'

'The same as anyone else. They roam

the prairie in big herds. Why?'

'That's what I'm after.' Wade poured himself another drink. 'Look, I've got some skinners and a few wagons. I've got some men who can ride and scout and I can handle most anything that comes up. I want a good scout, a guide, and you're the man I want. Interested?'

'No.'

'Why not?'

'Buffalo meat is Indian food. White men won't buy buffalo when they can get beef. If you think that you can get rich by supplying buffalo meat to the townships and the military then you'd better think again. It's been tried and it didn't work.'

'Who said anything about selling the meat?' Wade emptied his glass and produced a cigar case. He passed one of the slim cheroots to Big Jim, lit his own, and spoke through a cloud of smoke. 'I'm not interested in the meat, the bones, hooves or horn. All I want are the hides. Well?'

'I don't know.' Big Jim stared at the

tip of his cigar. 'Let me get this straight. You said that you worked for a big syndicate back East. Where do they come in?'

'All the way.' Wade sighed at the other's stubbornness. 'Listen. Fashions change and there's money to be made if you can get in on the ground floor. You've heard about that party of Redskins who went to Washington? Little Crow's tribe?'

'What of them?'

'Nothing, they went, they stayed, and then they came back. They aren't important. The important thing is that while they were in the Capital the ladies got the idea that it would be smart to own some buffalo skin robes. They want to upholster their chairs with skins, use them for rugs, have coats made from them, everything you can think of. It's a fad, it won't last, but while it does there is a big demand for buffalo hides.' Wade drew at his cigar. 'Listen. I'll provide full keep, flour, bacon, whiskey and tobacco and I'll pay every man ten cents for each hide we get. I figure that we should get a hundred skins a day, that's ten dollars a day for each man. I'll pay you double for acting as scout and guide. You should make twenty dollars a day, maybe more. Well?'

'Sounds like big money,' admitted Big Jim. 'How do you aim to get the hides back East?'

'We'll salt them and stack them on wagons. They can unload at the railhead and then come back for more.' Wade betrayed impatience for the first time since he had started talking. 'Look, this isn't a thing on which we can afford to waste time. There are others out on the same game. I've heard that Cody is collecting hides up north and others are moving in. Unless we start quick and act fast the herds won't be there waiting for us.'

'You think that?' Big Jim shrugged. 'Have you ever seen a buffalo herd?'

'Once, why?'

'There's close on a million buffalo on

the prairie. You think that you can wipe them out in a few years?'

'They can be wiped out in less than that time,' said Wade grimly. 'I told you that there are others on the same game. I've heard that Cody for one is killing over a thousand head a week and he's only one man. Don't forget the railways are feeding their workers on buffalo meat. The hunters are grabbing what they can, the Indians are killing them and every prospector and trapper is shooting his dinner on the hoof. Sure there are great herds of buffalo now, but in a few years they'll be cut down to size. We want to cash in while the going's good. We've got to collect the hides while the fashion lasts and the price keeps up. Do you agree?'

'I don't know.' Big Jim dragged thoughtfully at his cigar. 'The idea sounds good. How many men you got?'

'Twenty.'

'How many hunters?'

'Twenty.' Wade grinned at the other's expression. 'We all get in and kill. Then some drop out for the skinning and salting, while the others track down the herd. We follow, kill again, then skin and pack some more. I can get extra labour whenever I need it. I want you to locate the herds for us and then we can move in.'

'How you going to kill them?'

'I've got both Winchesters and Sharps rifles. The Sharps rifles are heavy-calibre buffalo guns. We can ride into the herds, shoot as many head as we can, and then get to work on the hides. After the first couple of loads I'll speed up things. I reckon that with luck we should be clearing more than two thousand head a week. That's two hundred dollars a man, four hundred for you. Big money, Jim, and not to be turned down.'

'No,' said Jim; he looked thoughtful. 'Where do you aim to do your hunting?'

'Out west near the hills.'

'That's Sioux country, you know that?'

'Sure, but what of it? The Sioux are on the run, they are due to go into a reservation anyway, and they won't bother us. Anyway, why should we worry about a bunch of savages when there's big money to be earned? The Sioux can keep out of it or we'll open up on them.'

'They may open up on us,' said Jim. He drew at his cigar. 'You thought of that?'

'I'm not scared of a few Indians, and I'm no Indian lover.' Wade stared shrewdly at the other man. 'From what I hear you've no call to love them either. Had a run in with them yourself, didn't you?'

'Yes, that was a long time ago, back when this place was known as Fort Henry. I don't love the Sioux, but I do love my own hide. When you start killing the buffalo they aren't going to like it. When an Indian doesn't like anything then he's liable to do something about it. You know that?'

'So what? The cavalry is pretty thick

about here and General Custer is fixing up a permanent treaty with Sitting Bull. They had a little trouble up there and a few hunters got themselves scalped. Custer will settle their hash for good when he gets round to it.'

'That's up in Montana Territory. Custer won't do us any good while he's up there. I'm worried about the Sioux, not the Dakotas.'

'You're too worried about everything,' said Wade. He rose to his feet and crushed out his cigar. 'Well, have I been wasting my time?'

'No.' Big Jim grinned and stuck out his hand. 'It's a deal. When do we start?'

'At dawn. I've been waiting for you to show up, I guessed that you'd tag along. Need any expenses?'

'I could do with some cartridges and whiskey.'

'You can collect them free from the store wagon. Anything else?'

'Not that I can think of. See you at dawn.'

'I'll be at the corral. Be early.'

Big Jim nodded and left the hotel. He checked at the livery stable and gave orders for his horse to be ready by sun-up. With nothing more to do he spent a little time and some cash sitting in a poker game and then, when he grew tired, he went to his room and fell asleep. He was awake before it was light, collected his horse and was at the corral well before dawn and in time for breakfast. He was wiping bacon grease from his beard when Wade showed up.

'All here? Good. Eaten yet? Good. Let's move!'

The party consisted of twenty men, twenty-two with Wade and Big Jim, and five wagons, one of which was the supply wagon and the other four the cargo wagons for transportation of the hides. All the wagons were drawn by mule teams, and each man rode his own horse. Spare horses were hitched to the backboards of the wagons, which were lightly loaded with salt.

The train moved fast and the first

camp was made around sundown some thirty miles from Homeville. The second camp took them deeper into Sioux country; on the seventh day Big Jim rode out with Wade to look for the buffalo herds. They rode mostly in silence, climbing to tops of mounds and scanning the prairie for the tell-tale signs of dust thrown up by the great beasts. They struck in a wide circle to the north, the wagons following the trail due west, and it was on one of these trips that Wade's horse stumbled and almost fell.

'Steady!' Wade jumped down from his saddle and inspected his horse's hoof. 'Must have kicked something, no damage though.' He looked around. 'Here it is, a wagon wheel by the look of it, all charred and rotten.' He kicked the crumbling wood. 'From the signs someone had trouble here.'

'They did,' said Big Jim, shortly. He stared about him at the browned grass and the low line of hills to the north. The place seemed familiar and with a shock he recognized it as the place in which the wagon train had been attacked.

'You know it?' Wade climbed back into his saddle and looked curiously at the big man. 'You've been here before?'

'Yes, about eight, nine years ago. I was wagon boss to a train of a dozen wagons heading for California. The Sioux jumped us and cut us to pieces.' He fell silent, then spoke again in answer to the other's unspoken question. 'I got away. A boy, a youngster, managed to get a couple of horses and he came towards me. I managed to beat off the Indians, jump into the saddle, and rode like hell back to Fort Henry. I was lucky to keep my hair.'

'And the others?'

'Dead. Most of them were dead when the Indians overwhelmed us, and the rest didn't last long.'

'I see. And the boy?'

'I don't know. We were riding like hell as I told you, and I didn't have no time to worry about anything. When I looked around a riderless horse was following me. The boy must have fallen off.' Big Jim shrugged. 'I don't like to talk about it.'

'They must have caught him,' said Wade. 'Those Sioux aren't too gentle with prisoners, are they?'

'I said that I didn't want to talk about it,' snapped Jim. 'Let it lie.' He rose in his stirrups and shielded his eyes as he stared northwards. 'See!'

'See what?'

'Dust. Away to the north. Now do you see?'

'Yes — yes, I think so. Indians?'

'Indians or buffalo.' Big Jim spurred his horse. 'Let's ride close and take a look.'

'Sure.' Wade began to ride forward. 'Now what are you doing?'

'Just checking.' Big Jim slipped the Winchester from its scabbard, levered a fresh cartridge into the chamber and replaced the cocked weapon. He took his pistol from his belt, spun the chambers, inspected the loads, and tested the firing pin. Satisfied, he rode after the buffalo hunter.

The dust wasn't caused by Indians. Before them on the plain, moving slowly as they cropped at the grass, was a great herd of buffalo. Wade stared at them, sucking in his breath as he made a mental count, and when he turned to Jim his eyes were shining with greed.

'Look at them. Let's get in among them and knock down a few head.'

'Do that and you'll start them running,' warned Big Jim. 'The best thing we can do is to go back for the men, let the wagons catch up with us, and circle the herd as we start the killing. Otherwise they may stampede and, believe me, there isn't anything which can stand up to a herd of charging buffalo.'

Wade fumed at the delay, but agreed, and the two men galloped back to the wagons and gave the men quick orders.

'Check your weapons. Two men stay with the wagons as outriders. Five men stay as drivers. Head north with all speed, you'll be able to find us by following the sound of the shots. We'll start work, kill as many head as we can and get on with the skinning. Get to us as soon as you can, and remember there's ten cents apiece for every hide we deliver to the railhead. Move!'

The wagons creaked as the drivers applied their whips to the mules, and great plumes of dust rose from beneath the wide, iron-shod tyres. The rest of the men galloped after Wade and Big Jim, testing their rifles as they rode, their eyes eager with anticipation. When they arrived back at the herd Big Jim gave quick instructions.

'Don't make a noise. We don't want to startle them too soon. Work your horses downwind and get in close. We'll do this the way the Indians do. Ride in the same direction as the buffalo, aim for the spot just at the base of the skull and fire one slug into each beast. Don't waste time following a wounded animal. Reload and fire as quick as you can. The herd will start running at the sound of the guns, so ride after them and get as many as you can. Don't ride too far, we don't want to waste time travelling a long way after a single hide.'

'Wait a minute,' protested Wade. 'Why can't we circle them in and force them to run against each other? That's the Indian way.'

'Sure, but when they do that there's maybe a hundred warriors and women on the job. They drive the herd towards a line of beaters, who scare the beasts back into a circle. But the Indians use spears and lances and arrows when they do that. Guns make too much noise and will start a stampede. Try circling that many animals and we'll wind up with dead horses and dead men.'

'Can't we cut off a few hundred head and do it that way?'

'Sure, but why? All we want is to kill them. We have fifteen men and each man has a repeating rifle. If they can shoot at all they should be able to get five or ten beasts apiece. We can try cutting off and circling later, but let's do it my way now. This herd is too big for any fancy stuff.'

Wade nodded, reserving his opinion, and he watched as Big Jim guided the men downwind and into position. They made little noise, but even so the buffalo, nervous as they were, seemed to sense that something was wrong. They lifted their heads and snorted and, at the warning signal, the entire herd began lumbering forward.

Big Jim fired the first shot.

He rode close to the back of a great bull and, lifting his rifle, aimed and fired in one swift movement. Before the stricken animal had dropped he had fired twice more, working the lever of the Winchester and nudging his horse forward with his knees. Around him the other men began firing, and soon the air was echoing with sound and heavy with smoke. Big Jim watched, then spurring forward he cut across the front of the herd firing and yelling as he rode. The leaders checked, bellowed, then, as the pressure increased from behind, snorted and charged forward as the hunters took advantage of the momentary pause to ride closer and pour lead into the hunched mass of beasts.

It was slaughter.

It was sheer wanton killing without sport or pleasure. It was a shambles done for nothing but gain. The reports of the rifles echoed from the distant hills and the bellows of the dying buffalo rang over the prairie. The killing continued until the herd, maddened and terrified by the noise, broke into a mad stampede away from their tormentors and shook the ground with the sound of their passing.

'Hold it!' Big Jim yelled above the noise and gestured to the other hunters. 'Let 'em go for now.' We can track them tomorrow when we've got these hides collected. He grinned at Wade. 'Well?'

'It was like shooting fish in a barrel,' chortled the hunter. He made a quick survey. 'Man! We must have knocked down two hundred head. I didn't know it would be so easy.'

'Killing them is simple enough if you've got a good horse and a modern rifle,' said Big Jim. 'Now the hard part starts. We've got to skin them and salt the hides.' He dropped from his horse and took off his jacket. 'Well, let's get started.'

His knife flashed from its sheath as he stooped over a dead animal. 'Get those men to work. We want this lot finished by the time the wagons get here. Hurry.'

Wade nodded and rapped quick orders. The hunters, eager to get on with earning their money, dropped from their horses and commenced the task of skinning the buffalo. They worked until they were red with blood, covered with it, their arms and hands steaming as they stripped the warm hides from the great creatures. It was hard work, so hard that they had time for little else, and even Big Jim felt that he had to rest. He sighed and straightened with a freshly-cut buffalo liver in his hand.

'Take a rest, Wade, you'll knock yourself out if you don't.'

'You're right.' Wade straightened and looked about him. Some of the men were still working, but others, worn out, were resting among the heaps of freshly-skinned animals. Big Jim grinned at them and yelled as he waved the liver.

'Cut yourselves a piece of liver and have a meal.' He bit into the raw flesh, chewed and swallowed with evident enjoyment. Wade stared at him with disgust.

'How can you eat that?'

'Simple, just put it into your mouth and chew, then you swallow, easy.' He took another bite. 'Bullalo liver is a delicacy to the Indians and they know what they are talking about. It gives a man energy. Want some?'

Wade felt in his pockets for a cigar. He lit one, stared up at the sky, then looked at Jim.

'Think we'll catch up with the herd tomorrow?'

'Maybe.' Big Jim threw away the last

of the liver and wiped his beard. 'They will run for a few miles and then they'll have to stop and eat. If nothing scares them we'll catch them tomorrow.' He stared around at the bodies. 'I'll hunt them down, but we won't kill any more until the wagons can catch up with us. We don't want to run hogwild on this thing, and the buffalo will keep until we want them.'

'We want their hides,' snapped Wade. He threw away his cigar. 'Let's get on with it.'

Big Jim nodded, and after yelling at the men they returned to their task. The sun climbed higher as they worked and they began to throw off their jackets and shirts. The pile of skins mounted and the stragglers were next to be attended to, the buffalo which had dropped while on the run and were so scattered from the main group. None of the men took any notice of the passage of time and neither did they notice that as they worked they were getting further and further apart. They had room for only one thought, the money they were earning, and so greedy were they for their percentage that they forgot all caution.

Big Jim was working with Wade, and as the sun grew even warmer, both men began to suffer from thirst. Big Jim straightened, glanced to where the horses were standing, and crossed to one for his canteen. He drank and passed it to Wade. The buffalo hunter tilted the canteen, swallowed and then, as he lowered his head, suddenly stiffened.

'Look!' he gasped. 'Look!'

Big Jim spun and narrowed his eyes towards the horizon. He took an instinctive step towards the horses, then as he saw that he was too late, yelled and pointed towards the west.

'Indians! Get your guns! Indians!'

Dropping the canteen he snatched the pistol from his belt and dived for cover.

'Fire,' he yelled. 'Shoot fast and often. Fight for your lives.' He turned a grim face towards Wade as arrows thrummed about them. 'This is it,' he said tightly. 'Those riders are of the Sioux. Shoot while you can and then die like a man.' Raising his pistol he thumbed back the hammer and sent lead blasting towards a painted face. Beside him Wade sobbed something and added the fire of his own weapons.

They didn't stand a chance.

Caught unprepared, the buffalo hunters were ridden down and slain like the buffalo around them. A little knot of Indians rode yelling across the plain to where the two men crouched down behind their barrier of dead meat, and as Big Jim heard the firing pin of his revolver strike against an empty cartridge, he knew that he faced death. Jumping to his feet he grabbed at a lance thrusting towards him, twisted, then fell half-stunned as a tomahawk struck him a glancing blow. By the time he had recovered his senses he was held prisoner, Wade at his side, and the battle was over.

A young Indian rode towards him

and stared intently into his bearded face.

'What is your name?'

'What's that to you?' Big Jim swallowed his fear and stared defiantly at the young warrior. 'You have attacked us, slain our men and now hold us prisoner. Why should you worry about my name?'

'Tell me!' Sam thrust his painted face closer to that of Big Jim. 'Tell me your name,' he repeated in English. 'Tell me! Tell me or die!'

'Ratford. Big Jim Ratford.'

'You are a wagon boss?'

'I was, why?'

'You stir memories,' said Sam slowly. He stared again at the wondering expression before him. 'Show me your arm, your left arm.'

Silently Big Jim held out his bare left arm. Halfway between wrist and elbow the puckered mouth of an old wound showed livid against the skin.

'How did you get that wound?'

'A Sioux arrow, eight, nine years ago.'

Big Jim stared wonderingly at the young warrior. 'What's it to you?'

'Do you remember when you received that wound? Do you remember a young boy, a very young boy who helped you to escape from the Sioux? You promised him a pistol and he saw his mother die. You remember?'

'Yes,' said Big Jim slowly. 'Yes, I remember. I have never been able to forget. He was a brave young lad, Sam his name was, Sam Strake.' He stared at the warrior with sudden understanding. 'You — ?'

Stone Face nodded.

8

Sam was very thoughtful on the ride back to the village. He had managed to stop the slaughter of the buffalo by attacking the hunters and burning their wagons, but the discovery that one of the men he should hate was the man who had helped him in his youth had shaken him. Not that he had any genuine emotional sympathy for Big Jim Ratford, the time-gap was too long for that, but up to now the white men had been unreal symbols, strangers with strange ways. Finding the ex-wagon boss had shaken Sam more than he cared to admit.

Big Jim was thoughtful. He rode with his hands pinioned behind him, his head throbbing from the effects of the blow he had received and the stench of drying buffalo blood in his nostrils. The fact that Sam was alive had shocked him, but not in the way his own existence had shocked the young man. Big Jim had heard of similar adoptions and his shock was in finding someone alive whom he had long thought dead. He had never forgiven himself for riding off and leaving the boy in those frantic moments so long ago now. Big Jim wasn't a coward, but he knew that at that time panic had overwhelmed him. He had acted like a coward in leaving the boy to his fate and had cursed himself a hundred times for not having slowed down and helped the lad. He had imagined Sam to have died that day, and now that he knew the boy was alive he felt a tremendous relief.

Wade, bound as himself and white with fear, spoke softly to the big man.

'That Indian seemed to know you. Is he a friend?'

'I don't know.' Big Jim Wade rode side by side surrounded by Indians who, both knew, would kill them at the slightest attempt at escape.

'How do you mean, you don't know?'

Wade was impatient with fear. 'If he knows you then maybe he can help us.' He licked his dry lips. 'What do you think will happen to us Jim?'

'I can take a guess,' said the big man drily. 'The Sioux aren't gentle with their prisoners. They may hang us over a slow fire or bury us in an ant hill and smear us with syrup. Then again they might tie us to wild horses or stretch us out with rawhide in the sun. That's unless they let their women torture us, they've a fine skill at flaying a man while he's still able to feel.'

'Shut up,' said Wade sickly. 'I ain't in no mood for that sort of talk!'

'I'm not joking,' said Big Jim seriously. 'We're in trouble and don't you forget it. They killed all the others, you noticed, and that means they are keeping us alive for a purpose. I don't like to think of what that purpose could be.'

'We weren't doing them any harm,' said Wade. 'I don't know why they attacked us in the first place. We're supposed to be at peace with the Sioux.'

'Tell that to the chief,' said Big Jim.

'I will and I'll tell him that the soldiers will be after us if he doesn't let us go. Maybe we can scare him into releasing us?'

'Indians don't scare,' said Big Jim. He stared at Wade. 'I didn't know that you was a tenderfoot. You talked big and seemed to know what you were doing. How long have you been in the West?'

'Not long,' admitted the buffalo hunter. 'I was East and saw the chance to make some money. I dressed up and talked big and managed to get a syndicate to back me. I came West and contacted some men who knew their stuff. The rest you know.'

'You poor fool,' said Big Jim without heat. 'You sure stepped into something.'

'Can't you talk to that Indian?' suggested the buffalo hunter. 'Maybe he will help us to escape. Offer him some trade goods, rifles, anything he wants. Talk to him, Jim, he's our only chance.' Wade was sweating with fear. 'What are you waiting for, man? Talk to him.'

Big Jim spat and remained silent.

The journey to the Sioux village took the rest of the day, and it was night when the warriors rode in with their captives. Low on the horizon the moon looked like a bitten peach and the stars glittered like a double handful of precious stones against the black velvet of the heavens. A wind, soft and sighing, rustled the undergrowth and caused sparks to fly from the fire, filling the air with tiny flecks of dancing redness which shone, wavered and vanished in a never-ending stream.

Sam led the way directly towards the fire.

Grey Horse stepped forward as he rode. The young warrior had returned with his bride from their honeymoon and was annoyed at having missed the fun. He glared his hate at the captives and spat on the ground before them.

Willing hands lifted them from their ponies, and two stakes, pointed and scarred, were driven into the soft ground before the fire. Wade and Big Jim, struggling, were lashed upright to the posts, and in the firelight their faces glistened with the sweat of fear.

'Sam,' yelled Big Jim desperately. 'You ain't going to torture us, are you?'

'Be silent!' Grey Horse stepped forward and his hand dashed across the big man's mouth. He had not understood the words, but imagined that the white man was yelling curses and insults. Great Bull, resplendent in his war bonnet, lifted his arms for silence and stood before the captives. His face was very grave.

'A bad thing has been done,' he intoned seriously. 'Stone Face and his warriors have ridden the warpath against the white man. He has slain those who killed the buffalo and burned their wagons. He has brought captives back with him. They are grown men and our enemies. They must die.'

'They must die!' echoed the circle of Indians, and as Walking Dog beat on his drum of taut deerskin they wailed and swayed a little from side to side as they sat before the captives and the fire.

'To the north the great Chief Sitting Bull has declared there will be no more war. He has signed a treaty with the white man. Many such treaties has he signed and all have been broken. Now he waits the yellow-haired one, the long knife called Custer, and they will make peace. Soon they meet in the place known as the Little Big Horn. The Dakotas will bury the hatchet and forget the place in which it lies. This news has come to me and it is heavy news.'

Again the shaman rapped on his drum and again the assembled warriors and women wailed and swayed from side to side.

'To the south the great Chief Cochise has sent word to the tribes that he will make peace with the white man. For long have his warriors fought and red is the ground of the Apache. Now the Scourge of the South seeks to smoke the pipe of peace and there will be no war in the hills and desert. I have spoken with the great Cochise and his words are heavy with wisdom. Listen to the words of Cochise.'

Walking Dog rose and walked around the fire. He rapped his drum so as to drive away the spirits of discord and purified the night air with gestures to the spirits of earth and air, fire and water. He danced the dance of appeasement and goodwill, looking like some weird monster as he swirled and danced in his mask and robes. The people of the Sioux stared at him and their faces were impassive, though their eyes shone in the red light of the fire.

'What goes on?' Wade twisted his head and glanced towards Big Jim. 'What is all this?'

'I can't make it all out,' said the big man. He grunted and called to Sam. 'Hey, Sam, what goes on?'

'Be silent!' called Grey Horse. 'Be

silent or you will die the death of a dog.'

'They know not what you say,' said Sam, and stepped towards the captives. 'Something serious is happening. While I was riding against you, messengers arrived from the tribes to the north and south. There is a big move to gain peace in the West. Treaties are being negotiated with Sitting Bull and Cochise. They both have sent word that they will not aid us should we continue to fight. Great Bull is appealing to the tribe to decide what to do. Be silent now, and listen.'

'These are the words of Cochise,' said Great Bull. 'To my red brothers of the Sioux I send greeting. For long have we fought one against the other and it was well to fight, for so it was in the days of our fathers and their fathers before them. To make war is good, for only so can the warriors capture wives and goods and gain strength and pride. To war is good while we are strong and there are none to ride against us. But things are not as they were. The white men have come to our lands and they did not ask us if they were welcome. They came with many wagons and many horses and we fought them and stole their horses and collected their scalps. Others came after them, many others and with them came the long knives and the forts of wood and stone. Still we fought against each other and that was a foolish thing.'

'Listen to the words of Cochise,' said Walking Dog, and his old fingers rapped against the skin of his drum as he kept the Council free from evil spirits. 'Cochise speaks well.'

'We are as an island in a swift river,' continued Great Bull, speaking the words of Cochise. 'We are as a straw in the wind. We are few and the white men are many. They come and none can stop them. They kill and none can prevent them, they rob and steal and lie and cheat and always it is the Indian who suffers. They have many guns and many horses and they have many, many soldiers. They fight and fight and fight and they never cease from making war against us. They do not stop to gather food for the winter for they have much food. They do not stop making war so as to hunt game for they have herds of cattle. They do not fear the time of the great cold for they have many blankets and warm houses of wood and stone. They fight and they kill. We fight and we kill. We are few and they are many. We are growing less while they increase from strength to strength. If we continue to fight then the Apache will be no more. We number but three hundred warriors and few more women. We are a dying people. We must make peace with the white man and live as he tells us. These are the words of Cochise.'

'They are the words of a woman!' Grey Horse sprang to his feet, his eyes reflecting his rage. 'He would have us beg for that which is ours. He would have us bow our heads to the white men. He would give our land to those who have no right. I say the words of Cochise are the words of a woman.'

'Sam!' Big Jim spoke with quick urgency. 'What goes on? Tell me!'

Quickly Sam related what had been said, translating the guttural Sioux into English and relaying the message and what Grey Horse had said. Big Jim looked thoughtful.

'Cochise is right, Sam, and the quicker these people realize it the better they will be. The Indians are finished. Now that the war is over all the soldiers can be poured into the West to keep the peace. The Indians are going to be granted reservations and they'll either like it or lump it. Tell them that, Sam. Tell them that from me.'

'No.'

'Why not Sam?'

'These are my people.'

'No, Sam, they aren't. You are a white man and you can't get rid of your heritage. These people are primitive compared to us. They are a dying race, a vanishing culture, and they must learn to accept that. How can a few hundred Sioux hold all the territory they lay claim to? How can they continue to hunt and trap on land which will support a thousand times their number if broken into farm and ranch land? Nothing can stop the settling of the Mid-West, Sam, nothing and nobody. If they try to fight, then all these Indians will do is destroy themselves.'

'Maybe, but what else can they do?' Sam glanced at the warriors and at the gesticulating figure of Grey Horse. The young man was trying to whip up rage against the idea of surrendering their rights to the white invaders as Cochise suggested. He was uttering wild threats and working himself into a furious temper. Great Bull and Walking Dog did not attempt to interfere, each Indian had the right to speak his own mind and none could stop him.

'They can come to terms with the soldiers,' said Big Jim. 'They can accept the lands granted to them for their reservation and learn a new way of life.' The big man twisted against his bonds. 'Hell, Sam, you're not dumb. You ain't no Indian no matter how you dress. Ten years don't turn a man from one to the other. You've fought the Sioux and fought well. They killed your Ma, remember, and Luke and John and Curt. They were decent, law-abiding people and they didn't mean no one no harm. All they wanted was to find some land and settle down. They would have been pleased with a few acres apiece and they would have built houses and raised crops and started a new life. They didn't and you know why. These Sioux slaughtered them for no good reason.'

'This land belongs to the Sioux,' said Sam, dully. 'They had no right to come into it.'

'Says who? The Indians? Well, who gave the land to them in the first place? And even so, what do they want with all this land? They don't grow crops or raise beef, all they do is to hunt the buffalo and trap game. They raid and kill each other and there isn't a tribe numbering much more than a couple of hundred people. Look at it this way, Sam. There are, say, half a million plains Indians, probably less. There are several millions of white men, some of them starving in the South. They want land and they have a right to it. They were born here just the same as the Indians and they can put the land to better use. Decent folk don't want to go riding and killing all the time. They want to build and raise their kids in peace. We can't have peace while the Indians might swoop down against us at any time and burn and kill. You know that, Sam, you was one of the settlers attacked in the wagon train. Did you mean the Indians any harm?'

'Did we mean them any good?'

'May be not, but is that our fault?'

'Yes.' Sam turned away as Grey Horse reached the climax of his speech. He listened without any real interest, his thoughts on what Big Jim had said, then as Grey Horse swung into the last stages of his speech he paid more attention.

'We must sweep the white men back into the sea!' cried the young warrior. 'They would herd us like cattle and rob us of our land. I say that this must not be. I say that we should ride against the long knives and kill and kill until they are all gone from the land of our fathers.' He raised himself to his full height, a proud figure in his war bonnet and warpaint. 'I have spoken.'

'Grey Horse has spoken,' said Great Bull. 'Is there any other who would speak?'

'I would speak,' said Walking Dog. The shaman removed his mask and looked at the warriors. 'Grey Horse has spoken, but he sees but one side of the tree. Cochise is not a woman, and if Grey Horse thinks that he is then let him challenge him to combat and meet him face to face. Sitting Bull is not a woman, he has proved that many times. For Grey Horse to call a warrior a woman is to speak into the wind. Listen now to my words. Stone Face has ridden against the white man and killed many. Because of that the soldiers will come and try to destroy us. Many warriors will die in the fighting and many empty tepees greet the rising sun. So be it, that is not to be helped. But the buffalo are going, and when they are gone then we starve. Stone Face cannot kill all the men who hunt the buffalo. Not all the Sioux or all the Indians can do that. So we lose our food and we die in the time of the great cold. Cochise and Sitting Bull have questioned the men who have come with promises of land. They have agreed to move into a reservation. There they will be given food and blankets, guns and cattle. They will raise the cattle and so have food. To gain a part is better than losing all. I have spoken.'

'Walking Dog is an old man,' said Grey Horse scornfully. 'His words are those of an old man. Are we children that we should nurse cattle?'

'Are the white men children?' said Great Bull sternly. 'They have killed many warriors and are not weak. Yet they raise cattle and no man calls them women because of that. Walking Dog is right, tomorrow I send word to the long knives and sign a treaty. Better to lose part than to lose all. I have spoken.'

There was some argument and for a time it seemed that Great Bull would be defied and lose his position as chief. Grey Horse, his face strained with anger, joined Sam as he stood by the captives.

'You are my brother,' he said shortly. 'My heart is heavy at the words of Great Bull. Join me and we will ride to the south. There I have heard is a great warrior who thinks even as we do. Geronimo is the name the Mexicans have given him. He fights and does not yield. He will welcome us.'

'He is an Apache,' said Sam slowly. 'Cochise expelled him from his tribe. Would he welcome the Sioux?'

'He would welcome any warrior with a gun and the will to use it.'

'And Many Smiles?'

'She is my squaw. She will come with us.'

Grey Horse spoke with the simple conviction of an Indian. To him the issue was plain, kill or be killed, fight or die, but to Sam it wasn't as simple as all that. The shaman and Big Jim had been right. Sam, despite his training and his Indian name, was still at heart a white man. He knew what Grey Horse could not know. He knew of the restless multitudes of the South and East, all straining to break westwards. He knew the grim determination of the white man and his conviction that he would never be beaten by a bunch of painted savages. Sam knew that the Indians stood no possible chance of ever winning the war; all they could do would be to harry and kill a few harmless settlers. No matter what they did now the Indians were beaten. Grey Horse was living in a world of dreams. Regretfully he shook his head.

'If you ride, Grey Horse, you ride alone. I shall not be with you.'

'Is my brother a coward?' Rage dictated the question. Rage and a burning hate that he should be thought to be at fault. Grey Horse considered that he had lost face when Walking Dog had swayed the tribe from him and he was almost insane with rage. So intense was his hate that he even turned on the man he had made his brother.

Sam realized this and tried to keep the peace.

'I am Grey Horse and Grey Horse is Stone Face,' he said quietly. 'For one to name the other coward is to name himself.'

'You talk like a woman!' snapped the young man. He stared at the captives. 'There are the hated white men. There are those who would kill the buffalo and rob us of our land. Shall they live while so many die?'

'Hold!' Sam grabbed at the young warrior as he stepped forward, the knife flashing from his belt. 'These prisoners are mine.'

'Stay your hand!' Grey Horse twisted,

the knife in his hand flashing as he swung away from Sam. 'I would not be touched by a woman.' He stepped towards Wade, the firelight glistening from his knife. 'I shall kill this man. I shall watch him die slowly, and laugh as he begs for death. He shall die as all the white eyes shall die. I, Grey Horse, have spoken!'

He sprang forward, his knife upraised, and Wade screamed when he saw the painted figure advancing towards him. Grey Horse was now all savage, he had reverted to the blood-crazed beast of the primitive and he had no thought other than venting his rage on the white man who stood before him. He did not think of Sam or the other warriors, or of anything, but his own hate and his own desire for revenge. He screamed his war-whoop and poised his blade for a ripping cut which would maim, but not kill, the helpless figure of Wade. Around him the Sioux watched with silent impassiveness. Such frenzies, which although not too common, were far from rare. Many Indians, either from drinking the raw whiskey sold at the trading posts or from tremendous emotional upsets, went berserk and then embarked on a private warpath of their own. When that happened nothing could stop them but time or death. They had to work it out of their systems in one way or another. Sometimes they slaughtered until exhausted, and at others threw themselves into the muzzles of roaring guns in their insane blood-lust.

Sam jumped forward and caught at the warrior's wrist just as the knife was darting towards the screaming Wade.

'Waugh!' Grey Horse spun and his knife flickered in the firelight. 'Woman! Die!'

Sam weaved, dodged, and sent his fist smashing against the jaw of the crazed Indian. Grey Horse staggered, dropped his knife and touched his hand to his face. He stared at Sam through eyes that were slitted with rage.

'Am I a dog to be beaten? I call you dog and coward and woman. I call you a lover of the white men. I call you enemy.'

'I call you brother,' said Sam unsteadily. Despite his outward calm he felt himself burn with rage at the insults thrown at him by Grey Horse. 'I call you *ananda*, my brother in blood. I cannot fight you.'

'I renounce you! I will not know you!' Grey Horse deliberately slashed the old wound on his wrist. 'See! I release your blood from my body. Dog! Fight me or be branded woman!'

Sam took a deep breath and glanced around the circle of Indians. They watched him impassively, but he knew what they were thinking. Grey Horse had insulted him beyond forgiveness. He had challenged him and Sam had to fight. Had to. If he did not he would be scorned and perhaps made to run the gauntlet.

He sighed as Walking Dog stepped forward with two knives.

9

The duel, for that was what it was, was to be fought before the two captives. This was unintentional, most of the warriors seemed to have forgotten the two white men, but the space before them was clear and the assembled warriors and women would have a good view. The shaman stepped forward and stuck the points of the two knives lightly in the ground. He stepped back and his voice was solemn as he spoke to Sam and Grey Horse.

'For brothers to fight is bad, for blood brothers to fight is more than bad. I ask you, each of you, if this quarrel cannot be settled without the shedding of blood.'

'I love my brother,' said Sam. 'I would not cause his widow to weep.'

'I have said the words which may not be unsaid,' Grey Horse snapped. He was trembling with rage. 'This man who was my brother talks like a woman. You all talk like women. I would have none of you nor of him.'

'It is well.' Great Bull stepped forward and stood beside the shaman. 'You have called us women, Grey Horse, and wish none of us. These are my words. You have gone mad with the desire for blood and have lost your senses in hate. You will fight and it may be that one of you will die. You may fight and it may be that both will live.'

'One shall die,' snapped Grey Horse. He tensed and his eyes glittered in the firelight. 'Words are like wind, they mean nothing. Stone Face will fight. I have spoken.'

'I would speak,' said Sam. He glanced at Big Jim and Wade. 'These men are mine. They are white men. I would not have them die the death of a dog. They must be freed so as to carry the word of what has been decided to the long knives.'

'You have slain their friends,' reminded

Great Bull. 'They will carry bad words. They must die.'

'I shall kill them!' screamed Grey Horse. 'I shall kill all the white eyes. I shall kill he who came among us, the one who wears the paint of a Sioux but who talks and thinks like a white man. I shall kill, kill, kill — ' Grey Horse clenched his fists and screamed at the stars. He was mad with the desire to kill and no man could stop him. He screamed again and tore at his naked chest, and then before Sam could move he had run towards the knives, scooped them up and turned with one of them poised to throw.

Sam ducked as the steel whined towards him. He twisted and turned and avoided the razor-edged blade with a mighty effort. He heard a dull thud behind him, a scream, and when he turned he saw that the knife, thrown with tremendous force, had buried itself in Wade's heart.

He turned again just in time to step aside from Grey Horse's rush.

Sam was unarmed and had to pit his strength and skill against skill and the rage-increased strength of the other man. Grey Horse had not abided by the rules of single combat, but the Indians would not blame him for that. They would think he had done a clever thing, and the accidental killing of Wade had caused many of them to chuckle. When two Indians fought in single combat the only rule was to win. How the victor won didn't matter. The fact that he had won proved to all that he was the better man. Fair play and elaborate rules had no place in the Indian scheme of things. Each man was his own law and though he could be scorned and expelled for unmanlike behaviour, it was rare that such a thing ever happened.

Sam could expect no help or sympathy from the watching tribe if Grey Horse managed to beat him. Not that he would need it; looking into the bloodshot eyes of the young warrior Sam knew that Grey Horse meant to kill the man who had once been his brother.

He rushed again, and again Sam dodged, feeling the kiss of steel burn his ribs as he darted to one side. He stooped, snatched up a handful of soil and flung it directly into his opponent's face. Grey Horse screamed with rage and shook his head to clear his vision. As he did so Sam jumped towards the slumped figure of Wade and with a great tug jerked the knife from the dead man's body.

'Watch him!' Big Jim called the warning as Grey Horse sprang forward, the knife in his hand driving upwards in a ripping slash towards Sam's stomach. Sam, still clutching his knife, grunted and spun aside. Quick as he was, the needle point slit the skin of his chest, and before he could strike back, Grey Horse had jumped away. For a moment the two men faced each other, circling as their moccasins felt the dirt, their knives held in the Indian fashion, like a sword, and their left hands held stiff and rigid so as to both give balance and act as a shield.

Steel flashed and sparks flew as Grey Horse thrust and Sam parried. They fought in silence, the deep sounds of their breathing echoing over the watching men, and from time to time the warriors would give a grunt of approval at some swift knife play or cunning parry.

Sam was handicapped by his desire not to kill the other man. He knew that Grey Horse was suffering from a form of temporary insanity induced by rage and helpless frustration. He tried to avoid the slashes and cuts of the other man while hoping to disarm him. Also, he had a second plan.

As he fought he managed to keep the scene of action at the post to which Big Jim was tied. As Grey Horse darted at him Sam risked his life to slash at the rawhide thongs binding the white man and, as he did so, snapped quick instructions.

'I'm trying to cut you free. Don't move for yet awhile. Get the circulation back and get ready to move fast if you have to.'

201

He grunted, dodged the lancing steel and felt the shock of the parried blow run up his arm. The blow enraged him and he pressed onwards, slashing and thrusting with easy skill, grinning as he saw blood streak the naked torso before him.

'You dog!' panted Grey Horse. 'You woman. You lover of white men.'

He was trying to inflame Sam and Sam knew it. He knew too that it was essential for him to remain cool. He laughed at Grey Horse, jumped back, and his knife sheared through the thongs binding Big Jim to the post.

'The horses are to the west of the village, beyond the fire. If I get killed make a break for it, they'll kill you for sure. If I win then maybe I can save your life.'

'I doubt it,' grunted Big Jim. He flexed his hands and stared worriedly at the weaving bodies of the fighters. He felt no regret that Wade had died, the man was a tenderfoot and a nuisance, and anyway, he had risked a worse death than that. In a way he had been lucky. Big Jim hoped that he would be equally lucky.

It depended on Sam.

In the firelight the two fighters looked as if they had been carved from mahogany and painted with oil. Their brown skins glistened in the dancing flames, glistening both with sweat and with blood from the shallow gashes with which they were both marked, Grey Horse moved in, his mouth twisted in an animal snarl, his eyes blazing with rage. He stepped cautiously forward, feinted with his knife, thrusting forward for the kill.

Sam had expected it. He allowed Grey Horse to knock aside his knife hand, then a split second later stepped to one side so that the darting blade slid harmlessly between his arm and his chest. Quickly, before the Indian could jerk back the knife in a cutting slash, he drove his knee hard into the other man's groin, twisted and slammed his knife hilt down at the base of the neck.

Almost he won the fight at that moment. Almost he had ended the conflict, but Grey Horse, shaking off the effects of the blows with incredible endurance, twisted on the ground, slashed at Sam's legs and, as Sam jumped in the air to avoid the knife, rolled so that he caught Sam's legs and knocked him to the ground.

Together they fought on the fire-warmed dirt, the blades of their knives flashing as each struck at the other. Sam had given up hopes of being able to win without bloodshed. He was now simply fighting for his life and he did it in the Indian way, fighting with every muscle of his body and fighting to win. He gritted his teeth as pain lanced from his side, twisted and managed to grab at Grey Horse's knife wrist, rolled as the Indian threw him to one side, and felt despair as his own knife hand was locked fast against the ground. Desperately he released his hold on the blade, wriggled his arm free and just managed to grip Grey Horse by the knife wrist as he stabbed downwards at Sam's throat.

For a moment both men strained, body against body, face to face, Grey Horse striving to bring down his knife and Sam fighting to prevent it from splitting his throat. He grunted as he fought against the unfavourable leverage, then jerking his head to one side he pulled down and sideways on the other's knife wrist. The blade, suddenly freed from all resistance, darted downwards and buried itself in the dirt.

Grey Horse released his breath in a hiss, snatched at the knife, then grunted as Sam kicked upwards and threw the Indian over his head. Before the other could recover, Sam was all over him, his fists pounding at his face and body, great hammering blows which gave the Indian no time either to snatch the knife or to strike back. Sam fought as a white man, punching with sure instinct. Grey Horse, an Indian born, did not fight with his fists at all. He could wrestle, use knife, lance or tomahawk, but had never learned to use his fists.

Sam, even though young, had had many a battle with larger boys and now that he needed it his almost forgotten experience came back to him. He knocked aside Grey Horse's weak defence, slammed his fists against the Indian's jaw, his nose, his eyes and his jaw again, and stepped back as the young warrior slumped unconscious at his feet.

'A good fight,' said Big Jim. 'Now?'

'Hold it.' Sam stood gasping for breath. His wounds stung as the air irritated them and he felt weak and unable to move. Walking Dog came towards him.

'You have proved yourself no woman,' said the shaman. He didn't smile, but his voice was amused. 'Grey Horse will not forgive you for what you did. It would have been kinder to have killed him. Now he will be pointed at and held to scorn as the man who was beaten like a squaw.'

'He is my brother,' said Sam. 'I could not have killed him.'

'And yet he would have killed you,' said Walking Dog. He looked at the slumped figure of Wade. 'He is dead. Manitou has taken his life. We are not to blame for his passing.'

'Does it matter?'

'It could matter much.' The shaman lowered his voice. 'Once I told you that the thoughts within you were not the thoughts of a Sioux. This even Grey Horse felt and that is why he turned on you. You are a great warrior, Stone Face, but the call of blood cannot be denied. It is wrong for a man to fight his own.'

'The Sioux are my people.'

'You are a white man.'

'I am a Sioux.'

'You are a Sioux,' agreed the shaman, 'and you are a white man. You are a man of both races. Always you will be a part of us and always you will be welcome in the tepees of the Sioux.'

'You speak strange words,' said Sam. 'You speak as if I am going from you.'

'My eyes are old, but they are not

dim,' said Walking Dog. 'This white man with the hair on his face, he means much to you?'

'We were friends,' said Sam. 'Many years ago now we were friends.'

'It is good for a man to remember his friends,' said the shaman. 'A friend can be warmth in winter, cool water in summer, he can be the tree beneath which to shelter and the weapon in a hand. A man should remember his friends.'

'I remember.'

'It is well. If the man with hair on his face remains here he will die. Grey Horse will see to it. Grey Horse or some other warrior who hates the white eyes. You know that?'

'Yes.'

'And that is why you have cut him loose.' This time the shaman did smile. 'I saw, and seeing said nothing. There are horses waiting you beyond the fire. Run and ride fast. Great Bull will talk to the tribe when the sun has risen and tempers have cooled. He will tell them that you have ridden to the fort of the long knives and there you ask for peace. This man can guide you and speak with the soldiers. He will give weight to your words. You will do this?'

Sam paused and looked at the old man with new respect. Like most of the young men he had assumed that the shaman was old and long past his prime. Now he knew that Walking Dog, together with the Chief Great Bull had seen more than others gave them credit for. They had seen what had to be and, seeing it, had decided for the good of the tribe. Sam felt a strange humbleness as he stood before the thin figure of the shaman.

'You are wise, Walking Dog. Before you I feel as a child again.'

'What we do is not to the liking of the braves. They will chase you and maybe you will both die. This you must risk. Tell your friend, the man with the hair on his face, of what you intend.'

'What's he say?' Big Jim stared anxiously at Sam as the young man stepped closer to him. 'Is he going to kill us both?'

'No. Walking Dog knows what I've done and he agrees with it. When he gives the word we run across the fire and to the horses. Then we ride like hell to the fort. When we get there you tell the commandant that the Sioux want to sue for peace. Forget the dead buffalo hunters. If anyone has to pay for them then let it be me. You just tell the soldiers that Great Bull wants to sign a treaty. Understand?'

'Sure. You coming with me?'

'Yes.'

Sam stared at the shaman and nodded. Walking Dog donned his mask, raised his arms and began to weave in a ceremonial dance. To the watching warriors it was the prelude to putting the captive to death by torture. To Sam it was the signal to make a run for it.

'Ready.' He felt Big Jim tense and he rapped the words. 'Over the fire, jump it if you can, and on to the horses. Now!'

Together they ran towards the fire. Sam felt the heat of it singe his bare legs as he jumped, then they were over, leaping the circle of warriors and racing towards the end of the village where, dim in the starlight, the forms of two ponies stood waiting.

They mounted, dug their heels into the flanks of the animals, and with the screams and yells of the Indians ringing in their ears they galloped off into the night.

10

The first thing Big Jim did when they reached Homeville and Fort Henry was to turn Sam back into a white man. He went out and bought a pair of trousers, a shirt, boots, jacket and hat. He cut Sam's long, braided hair and took away his Indian clothing. He took it all without argument, all but the medicine bag which hung around the young man's neck. That Sam refused to part with.

'It's my luck,' he explained. 'I ain't never going to lose it.' He spoke English with a slight difficulty, trying hard not to slip back into the familiar gutturals of the Sioux tongue, and Big Jim shrugged.

'As you wish, Sam, but you've got to walk and act like a white man. The way you stand now you look like an Indian in disguise.'

He stepped back and nodded at what he saw. 'You'll do. I'll get you a knife and a pistol at the store, then with a set of spurs you'll pass!'

'When do we see the commander?'

'Now. I've left word and he's waiting to see us.' Big Jim looked thoughtful. 'You know what you're doing, Sam?'

'I know. Great Bull wants to make a treaty. He can see that there's no future in fighting and wants to live in peace.'

'Peace?' Big Jim shrugged. 'Maybe. Well, let's go see the commander!'

The commander was an old veteran of the West and he heard Sam's news with mounting excitement. 'This is great news,' he said. 'With Great Bull sueing for peace, the Cheyenne and the Dakotas are sure to follow in line. I'll send an Indian agent out there straight away and go myself so to settle it. They'll have to go into a reservation, of course, but that can't be helped.' He smiled as he stared at Sam and Big Jim. 'You've done a wonderful job. Where are you staying?'

'At the hotel.'

'Stay there. Tell them to send the bill to me. I may be able to use you again.' He grinned again as he thought about it. 'This is wonderful. We were thinking of sending out a detachment of cavalry to bring them in, but if they really want peace we can save time, expense and lives.' He sighed as he stared down at his hands. 'Some people think there's something romantic in Indian warfare. I wish they could come out here and see it for themselves. They don't know the heartbreak and the misery it causes. Peace, almost at any price, is worth this constant bitterness.' He nodded in dismissal. 'Thanks again. Stay in the hotel and I'll let you know what happens.'

Back in the hotel Sam stared accusingly at Big Jim.

'You don't seem easy in mind,' he said. 'What's troubling you?'

'I never thought that I'd care about the Indians,' said Big Jim slowly. 'Not since that day when they attacked the wagon train and I thought that you'd been killed. I never had time for them or a good word for them, but things have happened lately to make me change my mind.'

'Such as?'

'You for example. They could have killed you and they didn't. Instead they adopted you and treated you right. Tell me, Sam, was you happy with them Indians?'

'Yes,' said Sam. 'Very happy.'

'Was you treated as if you was different?'

'No. Red Cloud, that's the man who caught me, and his wife, Laughing Water, tended me as if I was their own. They treated me better than my own Pa and Ma ever did.' Sam ground the fist of his right hand into the palm of his left. 'I feel that something's wrong somewhere. All this talk of reservations, what does it mean?'

'The Government grant the Indians a piece of land to use as their own.'

'Sounds good,' said Sam. 'Is it good?'

'Depends on where you're standing,' said Big Jim drily. 'From the white point of view it's good. We give the Indians a bit of swamp or desert which isn't any good anyway. In return we get the hunting grounds and hills.'

'Great Bull said something about food being given to the tribes for the winter.'

'That's right. An Indian agent will be appointed to look after them. He'll give them beef and flour, blankets and tobacco — maybe.'

'How do you mean 'maybe'? If they are to get it then they'll get it, won't they?'

'Sure.' Big Jim scowled as he stared through the window into the street below. 'Look, Sam, we've got to face this thing. The Indians are a menace. Even on the reservations they some-times break out and cause trouble. So what if a few cheating agents steal their food and swindle them? So what if they can't stand the farm life and fall ill? They're only Indians, ain't they?'

'You know what you're saying?' Sam strode towards the big man and Jim shrank back at the expression on his face. 'They ain't just Indians, Big Jim. Them Sioux are my people, as much mine as the whites are. So they've got their backs to the wall and are desperate. So they've agreed to a treaty and are going to trust the white man. Are you saying they've made a mistake?'

'They've got a choice,' admitted Big Jim. 'They can stay where they are and get wiped out by the soldiers. Or they can give up and move to a reservation.' He stared up at the young man. 'Look, Sam, I ain't against the Indians. I was, sure, but no more. I guess that I just don't like to see what is happening. I saw enough of it during the war. Those crazy slaves thought that the Union troops had come to set 'em free. They gained their freedom, sure, but then what? No one bothered to feed them, protect them, or care a damn about them. A black man stayed like that, just a black man. I've seen those poor people starve while food went to waste around them, and you know why? Because they couldn't pay for it, that's why. In the old days they'd have had it given to them by their masters. Slaves? Maybe, but most of them are a lot worse off now than they used to be. And the Indians are the same. So they get wiped out, so what? Is that worse than dying in a lousy reservation? The trouble is that they're beaten both ways. They haven't got a chance and they can't know it. Some of them think that all they have to do is to knock over a few troops and then they'll be let alone. They'll never be let alone. Never. They're beaten and that's all there is to it.'

'You knew all this!' Sam lunged forward, and gripping the big man by the shirt half lifted him from his chair and shook him like a rat. 'You knew all this and yet you let me go to that soldier and sell 'em down the river. Damn you, Jim, I've a mind to tear your heart out for what you've done.'

'What I've done?' Big Jim tore himself free. In the struggle his hand caught at the medicine bag around Sam's neck and jerked it from the string of beads. It fell to the floor and its contents spilled over the faded carpet.

'Sorry.' Big Jim swallowed his anger. 'I guess I'm all worked up inside. I used to hate the Indians and I find it hard to think of them as human. Sorry, Sam, think nothing of it.' He stooped and began to pick up the assorted stones and scraps of odds and ends from the medicine bag. He paused with a piece of stone in his hand.

'Where did you get this. Sam?'

'Get what?'

'This.' Big Jim showed him the stone. 'Where did you get it?'

'Someplace.' Sam picked up the rest of the things and put them back inside the bag. He held out his hand for the piece of stone.

'Wait a minute.' Big Jim stared at the

rock and pursed his lips. 'Think hard, boy, where did you get this?'

'I don't know.' Sam frowned, then as memory returned, he shrugged. 'I picked it up during my initiation. I thought it looked pretty. Why?'

'Do you know what this is?'

'Just a stone.'

'It's gold.' Big Jim let the piece of rock fall from one hand to the other. 'It's loaded with the yellow stuff. Where you found this there must be more, lots more.' His eyes burned with eagerness. 'Sam, don't you get it? I've always known that there must be a main seam of gold-bearing rock up in those hills. I couldn't find it because it was Indian country and I wanted to keep my hair. You know where it is, the place you picked up this nugget. You found a fortune and you didn't know it.'

'Maybe.' Sam took the nugget and dropped it into his medicine bag. 'It don't make much difference now, does it?'

'Like hell it don't!' Big Jim was

beside himself with eagerness. 'Don't you see what this means? The Sioux are sitting on top of a gold mine. When the word gets out the prospectors and miners will rush to stake a claim. If the Sioux try to stop them then they'll be mowed down. Sam, we've got to tell Great Bull to up stakes and move out of it. If he don't he'll be wiped out.'

'He's going,' said Sam. 'Didn't you say that they will have to move to a reservation?'

'That's right.' Big Jim looked thoughtful. 'Look. Sam, hear me and hear me good. You know where you found this nugget? You can find the place again?'

'Yes.'

'Right, this is what we do. We ride out and take a sample. We'll stake out the claims and register them good so that no one can rob us of them. Then, you and me will be rich. We'll have hit the bonanza without anyone knowing about it.' He stared at Sam. 'What's the matter?'

'That land is Sioux territory. Any gold found on it belongs to them.'

'Are you crazy? You don't think that the white men will allow the Indians to own a gold mine, do you? Hell, Sam, get wise to yourself. The first thing that will happen is somebody will start a shooting war, call in the cavalry, and when the smoke dies down there won't be no more Indians. The goldfields will be owned by whites and no one else.' Big Jim ran his tongue across his lips. 'Look, Sam, I know what I'm talking about. The same thing happened in Dakota, that's what all the shooting was about. It happened in Montana and in California. Wherever gold has been found the white men move in, reservation or not, and the Indians have to get moving or be wiped out. The only way you can save your Indian friends is to stake the claim yourself. We'll stake it and share it. I know the ropes and you know where the gold is to be found. What do you say, is it a deal?'

'I don't know,' said Sam slowly. He looked thoughtful. 'By rights this gold belongs to the Indians.'

'All right,' snapped Big Jim impatiently. 'So it does. But you'll have to mine it and hold it for them.'

He became serious. 'Look, Sam, think of it this way. Those Indians are going to have a rough time. If they had someone with a little money behind them he could make it a lot easier for them. He could bribe the Indian agent to give them a square deal. He could buy food and clothing for them when they needed it. Indians don't think about money, Sam, they don't use it and don't know what it is. They'll have to learn and learn the hard way. If we stake out the claim we can put half of the gold into a trust fund for them. Do that and you'll help them more than you know. Let it ride and the first prospector who passes through that way after the treaty has been signed will start a gold rush which will take everything the Sioux own and leave them to starve.' Big Jim stared intently at the young man. 'Well, son, what do you say?'

'Can we do it?'

'Yes.' Big Jim stared again out of the window. Below in the street a column of cavalry was passing. They were mounted and carrying full equipment as if for a war: with them rode the commander and a man in civilian clothing. The party going out to see Great Bull about the peace treaty. He turned to find Sam at his elbow.

'There they go. We'll have to move fast if we're to move at all. The claims must be staked and registered before the vultures move in.' He hesitated. 'Do you trust me, Sam?'

Sam nodded. He did trust the big man, why he didn't know, but he had recognized the ring of truth in his voice. Gold to Sam was meaningless. From his youth he knew the power it had over men and the things they would do to get it. He knew too that if the big man was right in what he said, the Sioux would be decimated and ruined by gold-hungry miners and prospectors. If the only way to save the Indians was to take their gold, then he would have to do it. He sighed and nodded.

'All right. We'll do it your way.'

'Good.' Big Jim moved towards the door. 'I'll order the horses and stuff while you collect your gear.'

'Jim!'

'Yes, what is it?'

'I'm a white man, Jim, but I'm part an Indian now.' Sam spoke with slow deliberation. 'If you try to cross me I'll cut out your heart. You believe me?'

'I believe you.'

'Good, now get the horses.'

Sam stood for a long time after the big man had gone. He stared out of the window at the busy scene beneath and yet, though he stared at it he didn't really see it. His thoughts were a long way away, back in the foothills with the Sioux. He thought of Red Cloud and Laughing Water, his adopted parents. He thought of Great Bull and Walking Dog — old, proud, intelligent men. He thought of Grey Horse, his blood-brother, who had turned on him from his hatred of the whites and from his fear that the old order was to change. The old order had to change and, unless the Indians accepted that fact, they would be wiped out within a few more years.

Staring into the street Sam couldn't know that Grey Horse would take his wife and ride to his death with Geronimo, or that Sitting Bull, when the treaty he had just made was broken by the gold-hungry prospectors, would ride the warpath again on a bloody trail which would end in the death of Custer and all his command. Sam couldn't foresee the death and degradation of Cochise, the Scourge of the South or the final humiliation of the Indians as, penned in reservations, they fought a losing battle to retain their pride and culture.

Sam couldn't know all that, but one thing he did know.

He knew that he would never forget the years he had spent with the Indians, and even now the urge to fling aside his hampering garment and to ride bare-backed over the prairie was almost irresistible.

Sam would never forget that he was a man of both races and that, though white, he was also by training and inclination, red.

He smiled as he looked at the scar on his left wrist. No matter what happened he would work and fight for the Indians, whatever their tribe. For he was their red brother.

THE END

On the run from the law, Vince M'Cloud and his gang decided to take over the sleepy little town of Arrow's Flight and use it as their hideout. After killing the sheriff, M'Cloud instituted a tyrannical reign of gun law, holding the town under siege. Anger simmered amongst the populace, and plans of revenge were afoot. But it was the appearance of the mysterious outlaw Abe Fletcher that really threatened to turn events around . . .

CAULDRON OF VIOLENCE

E. C. Tubb

Young Colin Bowman, orphaned after an Indian attack, is left homeless and alone. But the Civil War beckons and Colin, fighting for the victorious Union army, finds adventure learning the art of war. After the conflict, Colin's adventures continue, guiding Sam Curtway and his daughter Julia's train safely through Indian country. Colin learns the value of love, and when Indians attack, lives hang in the balance. Now he must settle old scores and move on to a new life.

LIGHTNING DRAW

Hank Fisher

He drifted into the Golden Nugget saloon in the ugly township of Come Lucky . . . Born in a wild and six-gun-torn West — the Cougar Kid was named after the most vicious animal that roamed the country. He was an ordinary cowpoke, but lawlessness and savagery had turned him into a ruthless killer. And now men like Jumbo Jordan, a rattlesnake of a man who runs a protection racket, will find no mercy when they face the deadly Cougar Kid . . .

THE LONESOME GUN

Ken Brompton

It's a fateful day for Orde Clemmins, foreman of the Star and Bar Ranch. A mysterious stranger — the spitting image of Luke Strang — is driving cattle onto his land. But hadn't Clemmins and his men chased Strang to Skeleton Desert and certain death . . . ? In fact, Luke Strang's son, Rod has returned to Arizona to claim his inheritance. But the odds are heavily stacked against him — a bloody shoot-out means many men will die before justice is done.

KILLER UNMASKED

Sydney J. Bounds

When Big Jim Stead is shot dead in the back, it seems Cliff Brent is guilty. But he escapes the hanging and takes the owlhoot trail for four years. Returning to his hometown, he finds his first love, Mary, believes he's the killer. Worse still, she's engaged to Greg Halliday, owner of the Silver Horseshoe saloon. Cliff is determined to find Big Jim's killer — perhaps then he could win Mary's love. But would revenge and his gun-skills be enough?

JUST BREATHIN' HATE

Dempsey Clay

When the Law went loco and charged him with killing his wife, innocent Jack Fallon had two choices only — run or hang. So he ran — to a strange lost valley shut off from the world and ruled by a cult of holy men who would prove more lethal than any posse could ever be . . .